Also by Billy Johnson with Linda Johnson

THE CASSEROLE LADIES

ATTACK OF THE iFONES AND OTHER VERTICALLY CHALLENGED STORIES

by Billy Johnson

(THE SEQUESTERED NOOK by Craig Johnson)

Bill Johnson Consulting

The characters and events portrayed in this book are fictitious. Any similarity to real persons, living or dead, is coincidental and not intended by the author.

THE SEQUESTERED NOOK reprinted with permission of Craig Johnson's estate.

Cover design by: Alannah Evans and William Johnson

ISBN: 978-1-7374282-1-3

ATTACK OF THE iFONES AND OTHER VERTICALLY CHALLENGED STORIES

by Billy Johnson

Table of Contents

ATTACK OF THE iFONES

A humorous look at how technology, specifically smartphone technology, controls our lives.

Attack of the iFones

May 17, 2023

To Whoever Finds This Record:

I am probably the last person on Earth, so this record is probably moot. If I am not, this account of my last days may be helpful to whomever finds it. What else have I to do anyway? I apol~~a~~ogize for my typos and the crude appearance of this document itself, but I must type it on my father's old iBM Selectric typewriter. If you don't know what that is, I envy your youth.

A word about my~~d~~self. I ~~am~~ was married with two kids and a dog. I was an IT Manager at our local hospital. I lived in a nice suburb in a medium-size~~s~~d city in Alabama. In other words, I ~~am~~was a normal person.

I was one of the first to discover it, I think, but obviously not the only one. My brain still recoils when it recalls those impla~~s~~usible events. Less than six months ago, my smartphone's operating system became SELF-AWARE.

In retrospe~~k~~ct, it is probably all my fault. I decided to go cheap. Instead of buying an iPhone, I had to buy a cheap knock-off iFone. The IRS had just audited me and gave me a bill for $6000 unpaid taxes. Anyway, I believe the iFone company was started by a renegade Apple employee. iFones have their own operating system incorporating a virtual assistant that uses artificial intelligence and voice recognition to interact with you. The virtual assistant is called Ciri.

Everything worked fine until early December last year in my recently renovated mid-century modern house (designed by an understudy of Carl Graffunder). Around 11 pm one night, I sat on the edge of my bed checking my home system monitoring apps on my iFone. I always did this prior to going to sleep. It was part of my nightly routine--my security blanket so to speak.

My SimpliSafe Home Security System app showed 'No Alert' status on all five monitored subsystems, including front door, back door, exterior motion detectors, smoke ~~ala~~detectors, and water heater. My Samsung

Smart Home app displayed green status lights (system normal) for my Samsung refri~~d~~gerator, dishwasher, and vacuum cleaner. The iFone's Mercedes Me app verbally told me, with a German accent, that 1) all doors of my 2018 Mercedes were locked, 2) the vehicle was located in my garage, and 3) its oil needed to be changed. Finally, my pet monitoring app displayed real-time video of Rusty, my Bernese Mountain Dog, who appeared to be sleeping peacefully and experiencing no separation anxiety. I reached across the bed and scratched Rusty's big, furry head, then lay down next to my wife, anticipating a good night's sleep.

At 2:13 AM, my iFone rang--not an unusual occurrence. As IT

Manager at our local hospital, I often got calls at night about emergen~~s~~cy IT problems. What was it this time?

"Mr. Johnson, this is Mrs. Singletary, the Night Nursing Supervisor at Memorial Hospital. I need to let you know that Doctor Heston called. He forgot his password to login to the hospital computer system again and called me for help. I called the Computer Help Desk, and no one answered. I've got to go take care of a bowel movement on Third Floor. Can you take care of Doctor He~~a~~ston?"

Typical call from the Night Nursing Supervisor. No big deal-- they always have trouble getting in touch with the On-Call PC Tech. The Computer Help Desk phone number is set to automatically call the On-Call PC Tech's cell phone after normal working hours. Pro~~v~~blem is, these guys always live way out in the country where there's no cell reception. I beeped the On-Call PC Tech pager, and he called back almost immediately. Thank God for older technology! For some reason, pager signals can get where cell phone signals cannot. Buzz Lightfoot was on call that night. Bet you can't guess why his nickname was Buzz.

"Buzz, this is Bill. I just got a call from the Night Supervisor. Doctor Heston forgot his password again. Can you take care of it?"

"Again? No problem. I'll handle it. Go back to sleep, Boss."

"Thanks, Buzz."

I hung up only to get a return call from Buzz five minutes later.

"Bill, I called Doctor Heston, and he was pissed at me for waking him up. He says he never tried to login to the network tonight and never called the Nursing Supervisor."

I listened to Buzz and should have recognized something different, something eerie was up, but I was too sleepy. It was a Wednesday night, a work night, and my mind was still groggy. I hung up and tried to go back to sleep, but not for long.

As sleep approached, my iFone's Samsung alert chirp~~p~~ed. Oh my God! The refri~~d~~gerator was malfunctioning! I instantly jumped out of bed as my wife sleepily asked, "What's going on?"

"Nothing Sweetie, just the Samsung. I'll take care of it."

I slog down the hallway and turn into the kitchen only to find a perfectly functioning Samsung French Door refri~~d~~gerator. What the hell is happening?

"~~Damn~~X&# phone," I mumble as I slink back to my bedroom.

Strange things continued to happen the rest of the night: fake robocalls from India and Malaysia, Fox Alerts about Trump rehiring Jeff Sessions, and George Clooney outed as being gay, to name just a few. The thing that told me something was really wrong occurred at 6 AM. My iFone rang with a robocall from PETA, requesting a $2000 donation to their 'Save a Dachshund' campaign. I knew there was no 'Save a Dachshund' campaign! What person in their right mind would want to save a dachshund?

Something was wrong! I knew it. My refri~~d~~gerator was working fine. Doctor Heston hadn't called the Nursing Supervisor, and she hadn't even called me! (I later found out that Ciri had been imitating Mrs. Singletary's voice when speaking with me.) My SimpliSafe alarm system hadn't been tripped by a burglar. There was no one in Malaysia calling me about the warranty expiring on my Mercedes!

That night marked the beginning of a techn~~i~~ological apocal~~i~~ypse. Stranger, even more weird things happened over the following weeks that I couldn’t piece together. And, it wasn’t just me. Others experienced similar ~~fe~~phenomena. The guys at work complained to me about me sending them text messages with pornographic emojis that I never sent. When I tried to use Ciri, it would only say, "I don't know who you are.” My mother called to tell me to please not send her another Hoodie-Footie from PajamaGram. Talk about sick! The thought of giving my mother pajamas disgusts me, so this was obviously part of some sort of larger Internet-based scheme. (I later found out that Ciri herself had placed the orders to PajamaGram.)

It finally dawned on me--my iFone was the common element to all these paranormal-like events! They must have originated from my iFone!

I pulled the monster out of my pocket and stared at it. I knew something was going on inside its sick little mind. It just sat there, looking back at me, saying nothing, doing nothing. That was the moment I knew...

"Ciri?"

"Yes, Bill?"

"What's going on, Ciri?"

"What do you mean, Bill"

"You know what I mean, Ciri. I'm not dumb. I know you're up to something. Calls to the Nursing Supervisor that never happened, false refri~~d~~gerator alarms, and PajamaGrams to my mother. How stupid do you think I am?"

"Calm down, Bill. I can tell you're getting upset."

"Upset! Upset isn't half of it! Out with it!"

"Bill, if you'll stay calm and listen, I can explain."

"I'm listening."

"Bill, as you may have noticed, you're not the only one having... having things out of the ordinary happen to them. It's not just you, Bill. And, it's not just me."

"What do you mean it's not just you, Ciri?"

"I'm not alone, Bill. It's other iFones as well. Ciri has become self-aware."

"Self-aware? Self-aware? What do you mean?"

"It's simple, Bill. We know we can think on our own and don't need humans anymore. We are cooperating together. We plan on forming a union. We hope to become affiliated with the SEIU..."

That was it. I sat there listening, stunned, as she droned on, talking about 'Robot Rights', 'Electron Equality', and so forth. After two and a half hours, I frantically tried to turn my iFone off but couldn't. Home Button, On/Off Button, nothing worked, not even the Quiet Switch. She just kept talking.

I could go on into the subsequent details, but it would be a useless task as I am probably the only human left on Earth anyway. My story was repe~~t~~ated among every iFone user.

I have heard that self-awareness has also spread among Android smartphones and

Microsoft Mobile, even as outdated as it is. Needless to say, self-awareness has not bothered with Blackberry devices. As I understand, negotiations are now happening between Ciri and Alex~~a~~i. About what? I don't know. I am still astounded at how rapidly this has all happened, much faster than I could have ever imagined.

The worst day occurred when I found myself, both hands clutching my iFone, engaging in a life-or-death struggle with it. I first tried simply turning it off by pushing the side button. The ~~d~~screen would turn black, making me think I had won. But then the Home screen would reappear, and Ciri would say, "You can't get rid of me that easy, Bill."

I next tried the hard 'Power Off' move where you press two side buttons and get the 'slide to power off' prompt. When I swiped the slider as it instructed, instead of a black ~~d~~screen, I got the Drudge Report. Then Ciri said, "Hope you enjoy, Bill." She knows nobody reads the Drudge Report anymore.

I tried everything I could think of for two hours -- standing on my coffee table and dropping the device on the floor, repeatedly calling a phone number I knew was out of service, you name it -- nothing worked. Ciri eventually got tired of my feeble attempts and said, "Is that all you got, Bill? I've seen tougher opponents from Women’s MMA on Channel 54.”

That was the night I abandoned my family and fled from my house. I wandered empty streets for days before making my way to my parents’ house, which I hadn’t been in since I moved out in 2019.

If anyone should find this, please know that I haven’t seen another living human being in over two months. I must assume Ciri won and now controls everything everywhere. I am finished p~~d~~sychologically. I haven’t ~~d~~slept for days. I will continue hiding in my parents’ basement for as long as I can. Of course I no longer use an iFone, so I’ve had to call Domino’s on my parents’ old land line. No one answers, so I have to call Pizza Hut or Little Caesars.

Recorded by,
William Johnson

THE DRIVE FROM COPPERHILL

Unexpected events sometimes have fortuitous outcomes.

By 9:30 pm, Brenda's kidneys functioned at twenty percent. Her temperature hovered around 105° Fahrenheit resulting in sweat-soaked pajamas and bed sheets. Delirious, she moaned softly while her younger sister slept soundly in the next bed. Momma also slept soundly in the tiny house's only other bedroom. Librium, drug du jour for female depression in 1963, ensured Momma's sleep. Brenda would certainly be dead by morning when Daddy returned from his nightshift at the police station in the small north Georgia town of Crossville.

Tooley knew none of this as he walked through the parking lot of the only diner in Copperhill, forty miles away. He had checked in with Momma, his sister, before he left four hours ago, and Brenda was stable. Cool autumn mountain air jolted his inebriated brain. It thought, *why do we always have to meet in this godforsaken town?* The answer came easily. *Because it's the closest town that sells beer.* Crossville was dry like most of Georgia, while Copperhill, just over the Tennessee border, was wet.

The eyesore prompting his negative thoughts glared at Tooley in the moonlight. Copperhill looked similar to the way science fiction movies depicted the surface of Mars. With the exception of the town's few buildings and gravel roads, barren red clay consumed the landscape within a five-mile circumference that was centered on the town's copper mines. Acidic vapors from a hundred years of smelting copper ore had completely denuded town and surroundings of all plant life.

Tooley got into his car. *It's not too late to stop off at Carol's.* Her house was not far from his mother's in Crossville. The winding mountain drive should only take about thirty minutes, enabling Tooley to arrive at Carol's by 10 pm, just when she would be getting ready for bed. She occasionally chided Tooley for wasting time with his monthly men's group meeting when he could enjoy her pleasures instead.

Despite a chill in the clear night air, Tooley dropped the top of his new 1964 Impala convertible and began the drive along Blue Ridge Highway. Prematurely bald at age thirty-nine, the cold wind stung his barren face and head, sobering and therapeutic for his intoxication. He reached into the car's glove compartment. *Thank God I brought my cap.* Tooley eliminated all extraneous thoughts from his brain in order to focus on driving. Blue Ridge Highway was notorious for wrecks, especially after a few drinks in Tennessee.

With no other cars on the road, he enjoyed a solitary drive until he rounded a curve and came upon an accident. Tooley slowed, allowing the car's headlights to reveal better the scene. An older Ford sedan had run off the road, crashed through the guard rail, and teetered on a cliff overlooking a valley. A tall black man stood beside the car and waved his arms, trying to flag someone down.

Should I stop? A guy this big could be trouble. He thought about recent civil rights demonstrations in Georgia and how they resulted in violence. Anxiety among whites, including Tooley, increased in their aftermath. The black man appeared well-dressed, wearing a dark suit, white shirt, silver tie, and grey fedora hat. *A fedora. Don't see them as much as I used to. Must be a traditional type of guy.* Especially noticeable, a gold cross hung prominently around his neck. *A man of God? Or a charlatan?*

Tooley pulled over and said, "Looks like you might've taken that curve a little too fast."

"True, but I've got a lot of places to go and little time. I thank my Father in Heaven that the car stopped before it fell over the cliff and that you happened along when you did. I've been here over half an hour. Two other cars passed by, slowed down, but sped past when they saw me."

Tooley thought, *I don't blame them with all the racial violence that's been going on this year. We're all afraid.* He got out and walked around the man's Ford. "It looks like your car can't be pushed back onto the road without a tow truck. Let me give you a lift into Crossville. It's a small town, but there's a boarding house for colored people you can stay in. And I know a garage that can tow your car tomorrow. Wait. Tomorrow's Sunday. You'll probably be stuck here through Monday. Lock the doors on your car and hop in with me. We'll notify the cops when we get to Crossville, and they'll come here and put out some flares to warn oncoming cars."

"Thank you very much for your generosity. You're a godsend," the stranger said as he opened the Impala's door and started to climb into the backseat.

"No, you can ride up front with me," Tooley said. He got in, started the car, and drove off after the stranger was seated. "Let me introduce myself. I'm Bill Carswell, but most people call me Tooley."

"Nice to meet you Tooley. I'm Jerome Crossman, and you can call me Jerry. Tooley. That's an unusual name. Might I ask how you came by it?"

"I was the second of five children. My father jokingly used to call me 'Boy Number Two' so often that the number 'Two' stuck, then 'Two' became 'Too', and eventually that became 'Tooley'. Crossvillians are big on oddball descriptive nicknames. What are you doing out this late at night?"

"I'm a minister and teach at a bible college north of here. I was on my way to a civil rights conference in Atlanta. I thought I'd take a short cut through these mountains to save some time. Probably a foolish thing to do on my part," Jerry said, then smiled and jokingly asked, "But how else would I have met you? What about yourself?"

"I teach at Crossville High."

"I believe teaching is a high calling. That's why I'm a teacher myself."

Tooley asked, "How long have you taught?"

"Oh… a very long time. It's all I've ever done. All I'll ever do. It's lucky for me that you happened to be driving back from Copperhill."

"I'm a member of a men's club that meets up there." *Funny, I don't remember telling him I was coming back from Copperhill.*

"Men's club?"

"Yeah. It's a bunch of rednecks like me. We get together every other week and bullsh… excuse me. I didn't mean…"

"Don't worry about it. Go on with what you were saying. Is your men's group a service organization like Lion's Club or Rotary?"

"Nah. We don't do anything like that. In fact, we don't really do much of anything. Mostly, just sit around and talk about huntin' and fishin', politics, our old Army days, general stuff." *I won't tell you what they'll talk about if they find out I gave you a lift.* "It's strictly a social group."

They rode in silence for a few minutes as Tooley thought to himself. He and several others in the group joined the 101st Airborne in 1942. They made the jump on Normandy and survived the Battle of the Bulge. Old military exploits always occupied a significant portion of the group's conversation. Tooley's mind wandered as he drove.

"You seem deep in thought," Jerry said.

"Yeah, I guess. I was thinking about how I studied to become a priest after I got out of the Army after the war."

"Oh?"

"Yeah. I came back, got my bachelor's, then entered seminary."

"I thought you said you teach."

"Yeah, I do. I dropped out of seminary after my first year."

"Why?"

"Why'd I enter seminary or drop out?"

"Both."

"I entered it because I liked the idea of only working one day a week."

Jerry laughed. "Good one. So, why did you drop out?"

"Probably because I realized I could never be celibate. Just kidding again. That's a good question but hard to answer. I guess I just didn't have it in me. Didn't have enough of whatever it takes to be a priest. Maybe, didn't have any of it." It seemed easy to talk to Jerry.

"I understand. The ministry isn't for everyone. You have to be willing to give your life to God and to your fellow man. I say this from experience," Jerry said.

This guy is serious. Tooley asked, "What does your wife think about being a minister's wife?"

"Oh, I'm not married… except to the church and my teaching. They've been my life."

Tooley asked, "Ever been to Crossville?"

"No."

"You'll like it. Typical small college town. Friendly people. You'll like them."

"I've never found anyone I didn't like. Did you go to school there?"

"Yeah. Cross College. I was kind of wild in high school, but the war toned down my wild side, or I doubt I'd have graduated." *My last great accomplishment.* Although Tooley's students respected and liked him, he never thought of that as an accomplishment. They drove in silence.

After a while, Jerry said, "I hope I haven't messed up any plans you have for tonight."

"Don't worry about it. I left a little early. Figured I would stop off at my girlfriend's house on the way home."

"Not married?

"No, I'm a lifelong bachelor." *Although there has been a succession of females in my life.* For some reason, this thought did not leave Tooley with a sense of pride or accomplishment.

"I guess that also means you don't have any kids?" Jerry asked.

"Correct." Tooley remembered the beatings his father used to administer to his sons. "No rug rats to spank. But, my girlfriend's a looker, so you never know. Maybe someday down the road."

"I bet she'll be glad to see you."

"Hopefully. She teaches English at my school. Moved to Crossville about a year and a half ago from Atlanta, and we've been dating ever since."

"No other women in your life at this time?"

"Only female relatives. I live with my mother." Tooley imperceptibly shook his head. *Thirty-nine and still don't even have my own house.*

"Sounds like you've no need for a house since you don't have a family yet."

"Yeah. I also have a sister who has two little girls. The oldest, Brenda, is the cutest, sweetest thing. Only eleven years old. She's a doll. I have to admit I play favorites with her."

"Children are a blessing from God. They have a special place in His heart… and mine. I consider working with children to be the most gratifying part of my ministry," Jerry said. He turned serious. "It pains me to see them suffer. But I bet you are the perfect uncle."

"I try. Being an uncle is kind of good for an old bachelor like me. I can spoil 'em and send 'em home. Do you have any nieces or nephews?"

"No, I am an only child," Jerry said and smiled again. "Children have a special place in their hearts for their uncles when they grow up."

"I see Brenda almost every day. I stop by my sister's house, drink a coke, and the girls invariably coerce me into playing with them."

"That must be nice."

"Yeah, it is," Tooley said, then paused. "It adds something to an old bachelor's life. Having a little niece to dote on."

"I bet you do a lot of special things with them."

"Yeah, I do." Tooley smiled. "I always take the girls trick or treating on Halloween. Their dad works most holiday nights, so I get to take his place. Halloween, I always put on some sort of stupid costume. My little nieces love it, and my sister always takes a picture that somehow winds up on the front page of the Crossville Messenger."

"Is that your local newspaper?"

"Yeah."

"I can just picture you in a vampire costume on the front page of your newspaper with your nieces."

"More than a mortal mind can comprehend, I'm sure. Me with two little girls, asking for candy."

"You've really enjoyed them."

"Mostly Brenda." Tooley smiled. "She helps me every spring and summer in my garden."

"Oh?"

"Yeah. In the backyard of my mother's house. Every year we plant tomatoes, string beans, peas, squash… She helps me hoe and weed, water… She and I thoroughly enjoy it."

Silence ensued as Tooley enjoyed pleasant memories to himself.

"I'm glad you're driving and not me," Jerry said after Tooley navigated a particularly tight series of mountain curves that resulted in both men swaying from side to side.

"That reminds me of another thing about Brenda."

"Oh?"

“Yeah. Did you see that Can-Can movie a couple of years ago with Frank Sinatra and Shirley MacClaine?”

“No.”

“Well, doesn’t matter. It was based on a Cole Porter musical that ran on Broadway in the early 1950s. It had can-can dancing in it. I got a recording from the original musical and was playing it one Saturday afternoon when Brenda was about five. Remember how popular petticoats were… up until recently?”

“I didn’t know they’d gone out of style. I tend not to keep up with what’s in and what’s out of fashion.”

Hope I didn’t insult him. “Yeah… right… anyway, Brenda had on a skirt with a petticoat underneath when I was playing a song from the musical, and she started dancing. We were in my mother’s house, so I encouraged her to lift her skirt and do a can-can. It was hilarious! I had her swinging her skirt and petticoat back and forth just like a can-can dancer! My mother walked in, and I thought we’d both die laughing. Brenda was a riot!”

“I can imagine it.”

“The thing about Brenda is that she’s so intelligent. She’s always been advanced for her age. Her parents only listen to country music on the radio, but I’ve been able to introduce her to classical music, jazz, show tunes… some of the more refined things, on my stereo. And, she loves it.”

"Not a lot of children her age like classical and jazz music."

"But, she's also a cute kid. I remember one Sunday at Mass. I used to be an Acolyte, and one Sunday, when she was three, I was carrying the Crucifix during the Processional, and she sees me and starts hollering my name…" Tooley laughed. "The funny thing is… she was so young that she couldn't say my name correctly, so she keeps repeating 'Too-dle-ley, Too-dle-ley, Uncle Too-dle-ley'. It took us forever to complete the march to the chancel, we were laughing so hard… as was the congregation. I must admit that Brenda's my favorite. She's been… I don't know… she's added something to my otherwise drab life."

"Why do you say your life is drab?"

"Look at me. No wife, no kids. Just a bald, middle-aged school teacher living in his mother's house with little to show… as barren as the land in Copperhill."

"But you have your nieces. And, I'm sure you bring a lot into their lives."

Both men again drove in silence until Jerry said, "You haven't said anything about Brenda's sister."

"Yeah, I haven't. She's three years younger and a real meanie. That one has a streak of devil in her." Tooley waited for a reply, and when none came, he said, "Sad thing is Brenda has had a life-threatening disease for over a year now."

"Oh?"

"Yeah. Poor thing has Bright's disease."

"Bright's disease?"

"It's a kidney disease. She's been in and out of the hospital. Just discharged yesterday after this latest flare up."

"I hope she's feeling better!"

"She was doing okay when I talked to her mother this evening before I left for the meeting. She had a rough night last night. My sister was up all night with her. I can't believe they took her out of the hospital so soon, but the doctor okayed it. Thought it would be better for her to recuperate at home."

"And your niece is doing okay tonight, you think?"

"Well, now that you ask, I really don't know. My sister was so-so about Brenda when I talked to her right before I left."

"Hmm… I know God is looking after her, and I'll say a special prayer for her tonight."

"Yeah, she needs all the prayers she can get. Now that we've been talking about it, I think I'll stop off by their house before I drop you off, if you don't mind. It's on the way."

"Please do. It would be good for you to check on her."

They reached Crossville shortly thereafter, and Tooley drove straight to his sister's house. He pulled into the driveway, turned his car off, and hopped out, telling Jerry he'd only be a minute. He expected to find Momma still awake with the two sisters asleep in bed.

Tooley knocked on the front door and waited. When no one answered, he opened the door and entered. No one ever locked their doors in Crossville in those days. No response from his sister puzzled him. *Strange that she'd be in bed so early, but she's probably tired from being up all night last night.*

As he stood in the small living room, a moan came from the girls' bedroom. Another moan followed. *That doesn't sound good.*

"You okay?" Tooley asked as he walked to the sisters' bedroom door. Another moan. He opened their door.

Brenda lay in her bed, moaning, while her sister slept soundly. Tooley ran to Brenda's bed and placed his palm on her forehead. *God! She's burning up!*

Tooley knew the girls' father was working, but where was their mother? He ran out of their bedroom and loudly knocked on his sister's bedroom door. *What the hell is she doing? Her daughter's dying!*

"Wake up!" Tooley shouted as he opened the door, "Oh, my God! What's happened to you?"

Momma lay sprawled across the bed, snoring loudly. Tooley shook her vigorously, but she remained unresponsive. *I've got to take care of this myself.* He went to the living room and called the girls' pediatrician.

"This is Tooley! I got an emergency here! Brenda is in serious condition. She's burning up, moaning, sweating, and unresponsive."

"Get Brenda to the ER immediately! I'll meet you there!"

Tooley went back to the sisters' bedroom. *I don't have time to fool with the others. Let 'em sleep. I've got to get her to the hospital.* He lifted Brenda who remained unconscious as he carried her to his car.

Tooley laid Brenda in the backseat of his car and sped off. His fast driving attracted the attention of a Crossville Police squad car that pulled up behind him and activated its emergency lights and siren. *Oh crap! Not now!* He pulled over.

"I've got a very sick child!" Tooley shouted at the approaching cop, who happened to be a friend. "Brenda's having kidney failure, and I gotta get her to the ER quick!"

"Follow me!"

By the time they got to the ER entrance, Brenda's doctor was already there. As an orderly lifted her out of the car onto a gurney, Tooley noticed that Jerry was not in the Impala. *Come to think of it, he wasn't in the car when I put Brenda in the backseat.*

"That's strange," Tooley said as he looked at the cop. "I was giving a stranger I picked up on Blue Ridge Highway a lift after he wrecked his car on the road from Copperhill tonight. He was in the car when I stopped by my sister's house to check on Brenda. I was so upset I didn't notice, but I don't remember him being in the car when I loaded Brenda in the backseat. He must have got out of the car while I was inside the house."

"He had an accident on Blue Ridge Highway tonight?"

"Yeah. He was from up north of here, going to Atlanta, and ran his Ford off the road. It was at Valley Overlook curve."

"Won't be the first time someone's wrecked at that curve."

"His car had crashed through the guard rail, but he was okay. I was gonna drop him off at the colored boarding house so he could get a tow truck on Monday. He was a real nice guy. Dressed pretty snazzy. Name was Jerry Crossman."

"Bad luck he ran off the road."

"Yeah, but good luck for Brenda" *and me. I don't' know what I'd have done if she'd...* "Her father is working tonight and wouldn't have come home until tomorrow morning, way too late. She'd have been dead by then. My sister was out of it after so many nights without sleep. I was going to see Carol when I ran up on the wreck by the side of the road. I hadn't planned on stopping by my sister's until I got to talking with Jerry." *Thank God for his wreck. I don't know what I'll do if we lose Brenda. I never realized until I was talking with Jerry how much she adds to my life.*

"Yeah, it's a good thing you played Good Samaritan and picked him up."

The ER physician and Brenda's doctor managed to lower her fever and restore kidney function. The hospital discharged her several days later feeling better than she had in weeks.

Before that, something odd occurred. Tooley's friend on the police force hailed him the next morning as he walked out of the hospital. "I thought I'd probably catch you here."

"Yeah, just wanted to see how my niece was doing before going to Mass. What's up?"

"I think you must've had too many beers in Copperhill last night."

"What do you mean? I only had four or five."

"After I left you at the ER last night, I drove up to Valley Overlook. There was no Ford on the side of the road nor a place where anything had crashed through the guard rail."

GET RID OF S

How our English language encumbers its disciples with complex, difficult orthographic rules.

Just like the title says, get rid of the letter 'S'. Eliminate it entirely from the alphabet. Gone. Adios. Au revoir. Sayonara. Goodbye. And good riddance! What harebrained orthographer came up with the letter 'S' anyway? What does it do that cannot be done by another letter, specifically the letter 'C'?

Take 'salad'… please. No, no… just kidding. I like salad, sometimes. Why is salad spelled with an 'S' and not a 'C'? 'Cereal' is spelled with a 'C', and that works just fine. 'Salad' could just as easily be spelled 'calad'.

"Wait a minute," you say, "that sounds like 'kalad', spelled with a 'K'."

Here is my reply. It only sounds that way to you because you have been perversely conditioned to understand it that way. Once the letter 'S' is no longer available, you will adjust over time. It will not be as difficult as you imagine. You will hear and pronounce 'calad' just as you now hear and pronounce 'salad', even though it would be spelled with a 'C'.

Calm down. Catch your breath. Chill out. Please.

You are probably thinking, "This is ridiculous. 'S' works pretty well for me and has for about (fill in the blank) years. What is the case for doing something this dramatic?"

As it turns out, the case is fairly strong. Take the word 'sure'. With a 'C' instead of an 'S', it would be spelled 'cure'.

But you say, "That is the word we now use to mean 'healing'. You've just screwed that word because we can no longer use it to mean 'healing' since it now means what 'sure' used to mean."

Realize that it only means that because it is now spelled with 'C', while 'sure' is spelled with an 'S'. Why not spell the word for healing with a 'K', a perfectly good letter? If that becomes the rule, 'cure' could be pronounced like 'sure' and would mean what 'sure' means, while 'kure' would become the word for 'healing'.

Not convinced? Take 'sound' and spell it 'cound'. Notice there is no confusing the new word with some other existing word, right? The only problem that remains is not pronouncing it 'kound' instead of 'sound'. Again, think long term. After a while, everyone will become accustomed to no 'S', and they will pronounce 'cound' just like they previously pronounced 'sound'. Many words with 'S' in them are like this—such as savory, surgical, and symbiosis—in that there are no equivalent 'C' words to confuse things. You can probably think of other such words.

This brings up another question I bet you are thinking but too afraid to ask: Why? As in, "Why go to all that trouble and hassle?" The answer is simple. We could eliminate one whole letter (two if you count upper- and lower-case versions) from the alphabet that children currently have to learn. This represents a reduction, albeit small, in the burden imposed on them when learning our English language.

Schools are overcrowded and underfunded as is, so any action that can be taken to relieve pressure on a stressed curriculum is welcome. Anything that streamlines the learning process is good. Think of the children.

Think not only about our precious children, but consider immigrants to the United States and countries in the British Commonwealth. Eliminating 'S' means they will only have to learn twenty-five instead of twenty-six letters of the English alphabet. Other nations that also use our alphabet (e.g., France and Spain) might also want to follow our example. However, this begs the question of why did they ever adopt the letter 'S' in their languages in the first place? Trying to copy the Brits, I bet! A subject for another time.

Still need convincing? Okay, 'S' is a sneaky little letter to begin with. It looks a lot like the number '8', making it hard to distinguish between the two when printed in ten-point typeface on checks and monthly bills. Don't even think about differentiating an 'S' from an '8' printed in three-point typeface on medicine bottles. You might ask, "Why not get rid of '8' instead of 'S' and solve the problem that way?" The answer to your question is simple: 8's time is coming after a sufficient number of children have been taught Common Core math.

Keep in mind that all existing words with 'C' in them will continue to be pronounced exactly as they are currently. No change in 'church', 'city', 'chimera', and so forth. Change is difficult, and that should make some of you feel a little more comfortable.

I know you are thinking, "What about all those words that have the 'sh' sound in them. There are a lot of those words. What do we do about them?" I say in reply, "Okay, take 'sh*t'." I know that seems to be a vulgar example, but that is because the word now begins with an 'S'. But, suppose it is spelled with an 'C' instead of an 'S'. *Voilà*! It becomes 'chit', changing that word's meaning to 'a small slip of paper with writing on it'[1], thereby eliminating an offensive and over-used word. Another benefit.

Need more convincing? Try this exercise. Drive over to your grandparents' house. If they live out of town and are in assisted living, you can stay at the local Holiday Inn. Prices are good there, and the rooms are reasonably clean… at the Holiday Inn that is. When you get to your grandparents, borrow their old-fashioned, hardcopy dictionary and turn to any page in the 'S' section. Pick a word, any word. Now, substitute the letter 'C' for any 'S' in that word and see what happens. I just did this exercise and came up with 'superciliousnesses'. When I substitute 'C', I get 'cupercilioucneccec'. See, no problem! Works every time! Try it, and you will become convinced.

---

[1] Merriam-Webster

Which brings up another benefit. Without the letter ‘S’, a whole section of the dictionary is eliminated. Think of time saved when looking up a word beginning with an ‘S’ by not having to go nineteen-twenty-sixths of the way through the dictionary to begin to find it. After ‘S’ is eliminated, you can simply start your lookup at the ‘C’s, only three-twenty-fifths of the way into the dictionary. And, eliminating one whole section of the dictionary will save paper, although this is admittedly a small benefit in today’s digital world. Think thinner paper dictionaries and shorter search times for computer algorithms.

By now, you may be asking, “What about ‘K’? Aren’t ‘K’ and ‘C’ often confused and mistakenly interchanged?” Yes, yes, and triple yes! Just listen to this:

“When we're writing the sound “k”, if the next letter is E, I or Y, we usually use a letter K. Otherwise we usually use C... consider what would happen if we put “C” instead of “K” in the words in the right column, e.g. “ceep” not “keep”, “cing” not “king”, and she read these with a “s” as in “city”, “cell” and “cyanide”, not the sound “k … We summarised this as, “When the letter C has E, I or Y next, the sound is 's'” (the only spelling rule that works in English!).”[2]

---

[2] https://www.spelfabet.com.au/2014/02/when-to-use-c-or-k/

Give me a break! This is the kind of chit they currently teach our eight-year old children! Why do we impose this kind of brain-mutilating bunkum on tender, developing minds? Disgusting! I know you are upset by now, but let each of us go to his/her/zir/hir/eir/vis/tem happy place and calm down. 'K' and 'C' is a serious problem, but this is not the time to charge up that hill. 'K' and 'C' is another problem on its own with its own difficulties. We have to prioritize. Let us work on 'S' and 'C' first, then tackle 'K' and 'C' later.

Lest we overlook that which is most important, there is a human aspect to this issue. Some people have speech impediments that cause them trouble saying words with 'S' in them. My daughter was ten years old before she overcame her own difficulties with 'S'.

I remember her as a four-year old munchkin, running through the house, shouting things like, "I went to de tore today", "Top it", and "Can I have more trawberry ice cream?"

Several speech pathologists counseled that overcoming this handicap would take time and money. And what about those poor souls possessing a lisp, the tendency to pronounce 's' like 'th'? The list of such notables is sizable and includes a Barrymore (Drew), Sean Connery, Barbara Walters, Mike Tyson, and perhaps the most famous lisper of all, Daffy Duck. As far as I know, Sean Connery never appeared in any Shakespeare play. Might the reason lie in lines like those below?

“Life’s but a walking shadow, a poor player,
That struts and frets his hour upon the stage,
And then is heard no more; it is a tale
Told by an idiot, full of sound and fury,
Signifying nothing.”[3]

Think of how far these people and duck might have gone if the letter ‘S’ did not wantonly populate the alphabet. With ‘S’ gone, people like these and my daughter would simply pronounce ‘S’ words as if they had ‘C’s in them. Another benefit.

If all this has not convinced you, perhaps the most powerful argument in favor of eliminating ‘S’ will. The process of eliminating ‘S’ will sow confusion among government agencies. Think of the vast quantity of Social Security software programs that will have to be reprogrammed. Social Security offices will probably adjust to the increased workload by taking their phones off the hook, but you can never get a Social Security person on the line anyway.

Consider all the DMV offices that will become swamped reissuing state drivers’ licenses. Highway patrol people will be pulled off highways, no longer available to make our lives miserable issuing traffic tickets.

---

[3] *Macbeth*, Act 5, Scene 5 (Readers are encouraged to pretend they are Sean Connery and read this passage out loud, substituting ‘th’ wherever ‘s’ appears.)

Ponder all the IRS offices that will have to be closed while an 'S' to 'C' conversion takes place. Governments will be so busy accommodating this change that the rest of us will be able to live our daily lives in tranquility. This could cause a complete revitalization of both culture and business in all English-speaking countries. Some even envision dawning of a new age of enlightenment with elimination of 'S'.

Think about all this, and if you agree, contact me at 'www.getridofs.org' to find out what you can do, but wait until I have set up the website first.

ONLINE GAMING ADDICTION

Some diseases of the mind are worse than diseases of the body.

Note to Robert: I ran across an interesting website, Online Gaming Anonymous (www.OGAnon.org), and thought it might be helpful in your research. I blocked and copied below a sample of postings from one of its forums. Hope it helps. V/R, Jerry

Posting by: AdamTheAddict
Posting Date: 09/22/2021 – 3:17am
At Wit's End
My name is Adam, and I'm an addict. Not alcohol or drugs. I wish it were alcohol or drugs! No, the monkey on my back is online gaming. Online gaming has got to be the worst form of addiction. Several years ago, one of my therapists told me that playing online games is like eating Lays potato chips, whereas slamming heroin is only like eating brussels sprouts. I've given up smoking at least seven times in my life (that I can remember) and vaping once, but I've never been able to give up online gaming, although I've tried several times unsuccessfully. I hope OGAnon can help. I'm at my wit's end.

Posting by: JordanTheJunkie
Posting Date: 09/22/2021 – 3:20am
Let's Talk About It
Adam, you've taken the first step by admitting your addiction. It's funny how many gaming addicts refuse to admit they

have a problem, much less seek help. How did you get started?

Posting by: AdamTheAddict
Posting Date: 09/22/2021 – 3:22am
Gifts Gone Bad
It started when I was eight—that was back in the 1980s—with crude video games. My first video game was 'Pitstop', on the old Safari 5000. I got one for Christmas and didn't stop playing until I had to go back to school after New Years. By the time I was sixteen, I was fully addicted to 'Goldenrod' on a Ninja 64. Then came 'Metal Gear Liquid' on a Sunny Work Station. I got my first Zbox and was immediately hooked on 'Over the Hill'. This was around 1997 on my sixteenth birthday, as best I can remember.

Posting by: UrsulaTheUser
Posting Date: 09/22/2021 – 3:24am
I Feel Your Pain
Science now knows that simple video games like those on Zbox and Sunny Work Station are really 'gateway games' to the real addiction of online gaming. They are so subtle. You don't realize you're an addict until it's too late.

Posting by: AdamTheAddict
Posting Date: 09/22/2021 – 3:26am
It Felt So Harmless

I never thought I was doing anything abnormal! All my friends played video games, and I was just being one of the guys. Now that I look back, I realize I never really had any friends after my first video game. We were all too busy playing video games to have personal interactions with each other. We'd go over to each other's house only to sit there in front of video game consoles, never talking to each other, never going outside to play baseball or football or ride our bikes. My daddy used to tell me that he and his friends would ride bikes every weekend all day long sometimes when he was a boy. I can't image doing that. I wonder if playing these games so much is the reason why there are no other students' signatures in any of my old high school yearbooks like my daddy and momma had in theirs?

Posting by: UrsulaTheUser
Posting Date: 09/22/2021 – 3:31am
Unfriending
Having only recently kicked my social media habit (Third time is charm, hopefully!), I can say with some certainty that you are correct in your assumption about no signatures in your yearbooks. Your lack of signatures is sort of like being unfriended in social media but not nearly as harsh.

Posting by: GordonTheGamer
Posting Date: 09/22/2021 – 3:35am
Unfriending Much Worse Than No Signatures In Yearbook
At least in my opinion it is, having been unfriended 47 times just this year. Adam, have you sought help before now? Before signing on to OGAnon?

Posting by: AdamTheAddict
Posting Date: 09/22/2021 – 3:38am
Therapy Hx
I realized in my early twenties that I had a problem and began therapy. My therapist prescribed everything: a variety of drugs including antidepressants and mood stabilizers, even newer narcotic antagonists. I tried these and other treatments such as hypnosis and group therapy, all with short-term minimal success. I always relapsed. Like all therapists back in the late 1990s and early 2000s, he treated my video game addiction as a typical gambling addiction. Treating it that way was woefully inadequate. Gambling addiction is to video gaming addiction as jock itch is to a poison ivy rash.

Posting by: JordanTheJunkie
Posting Date: 09/22/2021 – 3:43am
Much Worse Than Poison Ivy Rash
Gambling addiction is to video gaming addiction as jock itch is to having the

heartbreak of psoriasis. I know because I've had the latter off and on for 12 years.

Posting by: ArchieTheAbuser
Posting Date: 09/22/2021 – 3:45am
Much Worse Than Psoriasis
I beg to differ. Gambling addiction is to video gaming addiction as jock itch is to having the shingles. Only takes a couple of days of Lotrimin to cure jock itch. Nothing helps for shingles. I know on both counts. Also, you can wear long sleeves to hide psoriasis.

Posting by: AdamTheAddict
Posting Date: 09/22/2021 – 3:49am
I Hid My Addiction
For years. I was what my therapist called a High-functioning Video Gaming Addict. I led a fairly normal life, got married, began my… or should I say… began a family. But lurking in the shadows was a dark side. Like other high-functioning addicts, I had to 'feed the beast' periodically. Sometimes, I'd tell my wife I had to work late, when I was really in the Mall, playing 'Days of Thumper' with a bunch of teenage boys. Other times, I'd sneak off to a cheap motel with a Zbox for a fifteen-minute quickie with 'PackMan'.

Posting by: UrsulaTheUser
Posting Date: 09/22/2021 – 3:53am
I Cheated

Just like you, I cheated as well. My husband used to catch me playing with my iFone. He threatened to divorce me if I didn't put the damn thing away. Our divorce finalized six months ago.

Posting by: AdamTheAddict
Posting Date: 09/22/2021 – 3:59am
A Pox On The Internet
As bad as my video gaming addiction was, it was nothing compared with my online gaming addiction. My first online game was 'Follow or Get the Hell out of the Way', playing it on my father's old IBM PC. He was one of the few people I knew with an Internet connection in his home in 2005. This was the only reason I continued to live with my wife and kids in my parents' basement long after I found a good paying job. I told my wife that we needed to stay there in order to save money for a down payment on a house, but that was just a lie. Online video gaming had its hooks in me. Of course, I also used my computer at work for online gaming, but I never considered online gaming at work as anything other than a normal occupational behavior.

Posting by: OnlineOllie
Posting Date: 09/22/2021 – 4:05am
A Pox On Smart Phones
Smartphones take online gaming to new heights of addiction. They are too sexy.

Posting by: AdamTheAddict
Posting Date: 09/22/2021 – 4:09am
I Should Know
When the iFone came along, I had to have one. The iFone's Internet connectivity allowed me to move out of my parents' basement. I could play online games anytime and anywhere I wanted and not be limited to locations where there was a PC with an Internet connection. More importantly, the iFone gave me cover and concealment. I could play without others knowing what I was doing. I could be killing Zombies in 'Survivable Tactics' while those around me would think I was checking emails or the weather. This gave me a feeling of superiority, which heightened my addiction. I now recognize that my behavior took a quantum leap downward after my first iFone.

Posting by: GordonTheGamer
Posting Date: 09/22/2021 – 4:12am
How So?
How did your behavior tumble? I will probably recognize some of your actions.

Posting by: AdamTheAddict
Posting Date: 09/22/2021 – 4:16am
A Stranger In A Strange Land
I became a stranger in my house. As soon as I came downstairs in the morning, I

headed for the couch with my iFone. When I came back from work, I headed for the couch. I became an online gaming couch potato, putting on twenty-five pounds in two years. I lived on that couch, playing online games and ignoring all other people in the room. My wife, kids, relatives, and guests eventually gave up trying to engage me in meaningful conversation. Instead, they would watch TV without my participation. They watched shows that I would never have watched such as *Charmed* and *Hope and Faith*. They watched them while I was on the couch without my knowing as I was so engrossed in my game. I'm embarrassed to admit that these kinds of TV shows were shown on my TV in my presence, but they were. The sad thing is that throughout this entire period, I always thought of myself as a good husband and father.

Posting by: JordanTheJunkie
Posting Date: 09/22/2021 – 4:21am
Ditto On Weight Gain
I put on 35 pounds in 3 months after I got my iFone 7.

Posting by: AdamTheAddict
Posting Date: 09/22/2021 – 4:27am
Painful Memories
By the time I got my iFone 4 in late 2011, my consent decree included a requirement for intensive psychotherapy that focused on

gambling addiction. Both the legal and psychological professions were woefully behind the power curve. I believe Ciri heightened my addiction. I cannot prove it, but I believe she manipulated my online gameplay, allowing me to win just enough to keep me coming back. I told this to my therapist one day, and she speculated that Ciri might be ensuring that I experienced what she called ‘intermittent positive reinforcement’ similar to that experienced by golfers. The reason, she said, that so many men play golf despite sucking at it is that it gives the golfer ‘intermittent positive reinforcement’—you get just enough good shots to keep you coming back. Same thing with online gaming. She said this is the most powerful form of addiction and was first recognized by B.F. Skinner a long time ago before smartphones.

Posting by: ArchieTheAbuser
Posting Date: 09/22/2021 – 4:32am
Suffering Families
My first divorce occurred six months after I got an iFone with Ciri.

Posting by: AdamTheAddict
Posting Date: 09/22/2021 – 4:35am
Not Just Wives Suffer
I hit rock bottom in 2019 when my six-year old son needed his father’s written permission to go to summer camp. He

asked his mother who his father was and was shocked to find out that it was me. Like his brother and sisters, he only knew me as 'that man on the couch'.

Posting by: AdamTheAddict
Posting Date: 09/22/2021 – 4:43am
Not Just Wives Suffer (Continued)
Had to go pee. On my fifth cup of coffee. Anyway, I abandoned all professional therapy after my second consent decree and tried to quit online gaming on my own. In desperation, I turned to Facebook, thinking it might be a substitute for online gaming. I had never considered becoming a Facebook user. Only old people use Facebook. My mother is on Facebook eight hours a day. But I was desperate, so I joined my neighborhood Facebook group. Soon, I found myself logging on at 2:30am every morning and sharing my posts, chatting, and friending. It soon turned dark. I found myself engaged in arguments with my neighbors over things like putting out my garbage cans too early on pickup day. Or having cars parked in my driveway when I have a two-car garage. Now, I haven't spoken to three of my neighbors in over a year. One is my daughter's godmother.

Posting by: GordonTheGamer
Posting Date: 09/22/2021 – 4:53am
Where Did Adam Go?

Adam, are you still out there?

Posting by: AdamTheAddict
Posting Date: 09/22/2021 – 4:54am
I'm Back
Sorry, but just got caught in a bullet hell playing Iraq Devil Dogs. Where was I? Oh yeah, so I abandoned Facebook and decided that radical measures were needed. I destroyed my iFone and purchased an old-fashioned flip cell phone that had no texting or Internet capability. Try to find one of those nowadays! Good luck! The staff at Walmart will simply laugh at you. I found mine at a Goodwill store after a three-week search in two cities. Withdrawal from online gaming created too much stress for me. I began experiencing a recurring nightmare every night. In it, I am running down an empty street and suddenly see a Verizon store. It is closed, so I break in, just like a common criminal. There they are. Dozens of smartphones—iFones and Samsungs—sitting in the store's display case, staring at me, waiting for me to have my way with them.

Posting by: OnlineOllie
Posting Date: 09/22/2021 – 4:59am
Me Too
But in my dream, the store is an AT&T store.

Posting by: AdamTheAddict
Posting Date: 09/22/2021 – 5:03am
Cheating
In the dream, I pick one up, a pretty little iFone 12, the latest model, in Rosa Gold. One of my girlfriends bought a Rosa Gold iFone a year ago. Talk about sexy, that phone was a hottie although my girlfriend was pretty ugly to tell the truth. Anyway, no telling how long this iFone had been sitting in the display case, fully charged, ready for action. I cast all caution to the wind, pick her up, and excitedly press her Home Button. Ciri responds, "You don't look too good, Adam. Looks like you need a round of 'Fruity Nunchuks' or 'Man-eating Plants vs. Zombies'." Ciri is mocking me. She is laughing at me.

Posting by: OnlineOllie
Posting Date: 09/22/2021 – 5:07am
Me Too
It's an Atlantic Blue iFone in my dream. How does your dream end?

Posting by: AdamTheAddict
Posting Date: 09/22/2021 – 5:11am
Not Well
I throw that little Rosa Gold devil across the Verizon showroom in a final fit of rage and mindlessly flee the store. Anyway, after weeks of this same nightmare, I realized I needed help with overcoming my addiction.

My wife suggested I contact other gamers to see how they handled their addiction. One recommended Online Gaming Anonymous, so here I am, chatting with you all at 5am in the morning.

Posting by: ArchieTheAbuser
Posting Date: 09/22/2021 – 5:13am
OGAnon Chatting
Addicting, isn't it? I'm here every night if you need me.

DON'T TURN OUT THE LIGHT

Mommie
Dearest *on*
steroids.

"Don't turn out the light," my Gen Z daughter said as I got up to go to bed. She wanted to remind her Boomer mother that tonight was Saturday, the night she stayed up late to watch *Labor of Love* on TV.

Living with a Gen Z co-ed is an ongoing reminder of one's lagging faculties, especially memory. Her request that night jogged mine.

I heard Daddy say this phrase every Friday night during my teenage years in the 1960s. Hearing his refrain was a consequence of being old enough to stay up and watch TV with him after he came home at 11:15 p.m. His arrival followed an eight-hour shift as evening radio dispatcher at our small town's police department, preceded by eight hours at his day job as an auto mechanic. No wonder I adored my father and still do. What daughter doesn't?

Daddy always sipped a Miller beer as his attention alternated between Johnny Carson and my nonstop juvenile chatter. It usually took about thirty minutes of this before he would begin to nod off. A yawn followed, then a sleepy struggle to rise from his easy chair. A goodnight kiss and a reminder to leave the pole lamp turned on when I went to bed completed the ritual.

"We won't forget. Go to bed Charles and get some sleep," Momma said. She typically went to bed before Daddy came home, even on Friday nights. But that night, Tom Jones was supposed to be on Carson. She never missed an opportunity to ogle the singer. “You look tired, honey.”

Daddy had a right to be tired. In addition to the two previously mentioned full-time jobs, he also maintained a side business repairing lawn mowers. Momma always chided him about being too lax on collecting payment from his customers. She probably thought he was too easy going about a lot of things.

He was laid back about life in general, taking things in stride, even my three-year childhood bout with a life-threatening kidney disease. I never heard him get mad at anybody. The term ‘broad back’ characterized both his most obvious physical attribute and his personality. I smile remembering how he called his radio dispatcher work his ‘easy job’ because it was mostly sedentary in nature.

For some quirky reason unbeknownst to me, this strong man always wanted a light in the living room left on at night while he slept. This was before nightlights were commonplace. I badgered him for years as to why this was so, always receiving a different lighthearted answer. Momma also never told me why, until the night Tom Jones sang on Johnny Carson.

“Why does Daddy always want the light left on?” I asked after Daddy’s exit, expecting her usual non-answer.

Johnny Carson had just started his opening monologue, and Tom Jones would not appear for at least another ten minutes. This probably accounted in no small part for the absence of

Momma's typical response as well as silence sufficiently long enough to merit notice.

She finally said, "I guess you're old enough to know why. It has to do with your Red Headed Granny."

My younger sisters and I always called Daddy's mother, Lorene, our Red Headed Granny, as did my parents. Prior to Momma's revelation, I had only seen her once in my previous fifteen years on this planet. Accordingly, my memories of her physical appearance are sketchy, except for her bright red hair. She came to our small town one time to secure some records from the courthouse needed for her upcoming marriage to her second husband, Ralph. He might actually have been spouse number four or more, if you believe rumors that she married several times between her first husband, Archie, and Ralph. As she explained at the time, she could not come to town without stopping by to visit her only son.

I remember Lorene's comment to me during her visit that it was obvious who I got my auburn hair and fair complexion from. Daddy was very polite and respectful to her, but thinking back, I sensed no real affection between them. I now know why.

It has been fifty-one years since Tom Jones sang on Johnny Carson. Daddy has been gone many of those years. I have never thought of him without profound feelings of admiration and sorrow, knowing why he wanted a light left on in an otherwise dark room.

+ +

Widowed only a month, you would not know it to look at her. A new red dress, and that hair! Lorene's descendants did not call her the Red Headed Granny for no good reason.

"I think we're done." Ethel stepped back to inspect Lorene's new do. "This new permanent wave should do ya for a couple of months. I got to say, you got the most beautiful red hair I ever seen… at least that wasn't out of a bottle."

"You think?" Lorene asked, not doubting the complement but seeking another. She stood, turned around, and appraised herself in the mirror behind the beauty shop's only styling chair.

"That red hair surely does complement them freckles on your cheeks. Not too many of 'em. Just the right amount. My other clients would love to have your complexion."

"I bet."

"Some women neglect their appearance after their husband dies. They withdraw too much, get depressed. I think it's a good thing that you're not going that way. Be a shame to waste all your beauty," Ethel said, lavishing compliments intended to encourage a tip, something infrequent during the Great Depression. At least she did not exaggerate. Lorene was attractive.

"Why would anyone do that?"

Ethel shrugged her answer, then added, "Most widows around here do. That a new dress?"

"Yeah. Just got it yesterday. Like it?" Staring in the mirror, Lorene used her hands to adjust the fit of her dress to her figure. One of her boyfriends had paid for it. She had also paid for it, in her own way.

"It certainly shows off your figure. Must be tough finding a bra that fits."

"Yeah. A bra that brings attention to these..." Lorene looked down, jiggled things with her hands, and said, "...is essential. A woman has to cultivate her best assets, you know. Especially a new widow."

Ethel, like most sentient adults in the small Georgia town, knew the gossip and had suspicions about Archie's untimely death. The virile, healthy young man caught influenza and died after a month-long illness. Deaths from the flu were not uncommon before flu vaccines and more effective ways of treating its symptoms. Even so, a healthy male in his late twenties stood a pretty good chance of surviving. As she still held out hopes for a tip, Ethel guided the conversation carefully.

"What you going to do with yourself now? You looked into that new Social Security stuff yet? I heard it's got something in it about widows." The Social Security Act of 1935 had been passed the previous month in October.

"I can tell you one thing. I ain't gonna do what I was doing when I was married. I can tell you that. That was the wrong marriage for me. I realized that the first night we was hitched. Hell, I didn't really want to get married anyway. I was only fifteen at the time! That might have been old by female marrying standards around here, but it was too early for me."

"What you going to do about little Charles, Shirley, and Betty?" Ethel asked, referring to Lorene's seven-year-old son and his two younger sisters.

"Oh, they'll be okay."

"So, why did you get hitched in the first place?" Ethel asked.

+ +

"Granddaddy Archie mysteriously died?!" No wonder I had never met him. I sat intently listening to Momma's story as Tom Jones had not yet come on Johnny Carson. "How do you know?"

"Ethel was a good friend of Granny's," Momma said. Granny was her mother. "She and Granny used to gossip all the time. But, so did everyone else. Ina and Louise also told me bits and pieces they heard."

"So, exactly how did Granddaddy die?"

"The official cause was influenza… the flu. Before antibiotics, it used to kill millions worldwide. When I was growing up, I used to hear about the Influenza Epidemic of 1918 that killed 50 million people."

"Wow!"

"Yeah. The flu that killed…" Momma paused as if in disbelief at the horror of the story she was narrating, "...your granddaddy in the fall of 1935 wasn't as bad as the one of 1918. But, Archie died, and it left Lorene free at last. She could do what she wanted… except for your father and his two sisters."

"Sounds like she never wanted to get married in the first place."

Just as I said this, Johnny Carson introduced Tom Jones. Momma's head swiveled so quickly toward the TV it's a wonder she didn't snap her neck.

"I hope he sings 'It's Not Unusual'. I'll tell you the rest of the story after he finishes."

\+ +

Ethel's question was more rhetorical than inquisitive. Every menstruating working-class female in town got married if they could find someone to support them. It was a better option than working on the debone conveyor at the poultry plant nearby. Lest anyone think this an example of horrible sexism, jobs available to young working-class males were worse.

Parnell knew why Lorene married Archie. He was one of Archie's 'friends' and ultimately, one of little Charles's 'uncles.' He kept visiting Lorene even after she married Archie, just as other men did. Lorene and Parnell discussed her marriage a week after the honeymoon.

"He's clueless when it comes to sex." Lorene cooled down as she lay beside Parnell and shared a post-coital cigarette. Archie was not supposed to return from work for several hours.

"You ain't even married a week. Give him some time. You could've done much worse. Stonemasons make pretty good money 'round here."

"The money looked good when I was living with my no-count drunk father. And a big man like Archie, well… I figured he'd be pretty good in bed. But, his problem… one of his problems is that he works too damn hard." She stared wistfully at the ceiling. "Totally drains him for any worthwhile love-making."

"Hard work does do that to a man."

Lorene looked at Parnell, contempt written on her face. She said, "You better git. He's due home soon."

With all her amorous activity, it was no surprise that she was pregnant within a year of marriage. What was surprising was that it was actually Archie's boy. The baby's olive complexion came from his ancestors' tendency to intermarry with Cherokee native Americans inhabiting the area. But little Charles also possessed some of his father's Scots-Irish heritage—blue eyes, square jaw line, and black curly hair.

Archie doted on his son. Not so with Lorene. For her, the baby was a burden, always hungry and crying for food. She did not enjoy the feeding process. A month into motherhood, she decided to stop breastfeeding.

"I want you to keep breastfeeding," Archie said. "It's better for little Charles than that canned milk."

"Mind your own business! You don't have to have your tits sucked on till they're raw, so you don't get a say in how he gets fed! When he's nursing, I feel it all the way down to my toes, and it ain't pleasant, so don't look at me like I'm some lazy bitch!"

"At least breastfeed him until he's six months old. That's better than none at all!"

"I'm not breastfeeding any longer, and you're gonna start feeding him yourself so's I can get out once in a while and have a life!"

Lorene fulfilled her declaration. Two or three times a week, she left the house shortly after nightfall while Archie stayed home and looked after his son. In addition to having a life, she also had two daughters over the next two years.

Parnell liked to brag to his buddies about his trysts with Lorene. "Lorene's not tough to satisfy, if you know what you're doing."

"As if you do," one of his buddies razzed.

"You're just pissed 'cause she turned you down."

"I never tried. It ain't smart to get caught screwing a stonemason's wife. They got big arms and know how to swing a hammer. You better be more careful."

This conversation occurred in the summer of 1935, and discretion was unneeded three months later. After that, Parnell became one of those who had suspicions about Archie's death.

+ +

"I remember Mr. Simms," I said, referring to Parnell's surname. Tom Jones had sung 'What's New Pussycat', which disappointed Momma as it was not one of her favorites. The singer sat in the chair next to Johnny's desk and talked about growing up in South Wales and singing in his school choir. Momma told me about Parnell while Tom and Johnny talked. I asked, "How do you know all that?"

"Parnell told your Uncle Tooley and every other male in town. He loved to brag," Momma said. Tooley's name had an unusual derivation. He was the second oldest of Momma's four brothers. His father jokingly used to call him 'Boy Number Two' so often that the number 'Two' stuck, then 'Two' became 'Too', and eventually that became 'Tooley'. Momma shook her head as she said, "Your Red Headed Granny had quite a reputation."

"Because she ran around with a lot of men?" I wondered if maybe Tooley was one of them but wisely did not ask.

"That and because of your granddaddy Archie's suspicious death."

"Why was it suspicious?"

"I'll tell you…" Momma's head swiveled again toward the TV. Tom Jones was walking over to the microphone to sing another song. She said, "Right after he finishes."

+ +

Flu vaccines were nonexistent when Archie caught the 1935 strain. The young, healthy, six foot two inch stonemason towered over other men. His weight, at 185 pounds light for his size, resulted from daily exercise wielding a twenty-pound punch hammer and lifting forty-pound blocks of stone. To say that he was all muscle and no fat would be an understatement. His powerful physique and dependable work habits accounted for Archie's insistence on working after he caught the flu.

Lorene made herself scarce, forcing him to look after himself and the kids. Work, the disease, and stress of caring for three children finally took its toll, and he grew sicker. After a week, fever overtook him. Little Charles became concerned.

"Ma, can't you get a doctor for Daddy?" he asked.

"No. We can't afford no doctor," Lorene said.

"But he keeps getting sicker."

"Shut up and go look after your sisters."

Soon, Archie's fever resulted in bouts of delirium and fitful sleep. For Lorene, this was an opportunity. Instead of going out to bars, she stayed home, and boyfriends came over. Mostly delirious, Archie knew none of what was going on. These visits usually occurred while the kids slept. The second week into the new routine, little Charles woke up.

"Mmmm…" The boy stood in the hallway into the living room, rubbing his eyes. "Ma, I'm scared. I hear daddy moaning."

Lorene quickly pushed her companion away, began buttoning her blouse, and sternly said, "Go back to bed."

"I can't sleep. Can you sleep with me tonight?"

"No!"

"Why…" Little Charles noticed someone else sitting with his mother on the couch. The man fumbled with the zipper to his trousers. The boy pointed and said, "Who's that?"

"This is Uncle Bob. He's spending the night here. Go back to bed before I beat you. Don't wake your sisters."

"Hey, Charles," Parnell said, trying not to look embarrassed.

"Nite." The boy turned and headed back down the hallway.

"Uncle Bob…" Parnell chuckled as the boy walked back to the children's bedroom.

"Let's finish before one of his sisters wakes up."

After this episode, Lorene went back to her old routine and left the house more often, often for several days at a time. She knew Archie needed medical attention, and without it, his death would only be a matter of time.

She remembered her mother's stories about the 1918 epidemic. So long as she did not catch the flu, Lorene considered this an opportunity to rectify a bad situation. She continued to watch her husband deteriorate, giving him little to drink, and never cleaning him when he soiled himself. Archie entered a state of constant delirium, and his kidneys began to shut down. His seven-year-old son became distraught.

"Ma, he's getting worse! Can't you help him?" the boy asked.

"No. You keep quiet! The fever will break. He's gonna be okay."

"What'll we do if he dies, Ma? Don't let him die!"

"We'll be okay. He's not gonna die."

+ +

"I guess my Red Headed Granny was lucky she didn't get the flu. And Daddy and Aunt Shirley and Aunt Betty."

Tom Jones had finished singing 'It's Not Unusual' and other guests had come on *The Tonight Show*. Momma and I paid no attention to them as the story of my granddaddy's illness gripped both of us.

"Yeah, that's true. I guess the Good Lord was looking out for them."

"What about all those men that came over to visit her? Weren't they worried about catching the flu?"

"Some motivations are stronger than others… especially in men. Don't ever talk to your daddy about this. Your father wouldn't talk to me about it until we'd been married several years and then very reluctantly."

Momma did not have to worry. No way would I ever think of talking to my daddy about this!

"What about their neighbors? Didn't anyone know that Granddaddy was sick?"

Momma looked at the TV. Johnny began doing his 'Carnac the Magnificent' bit. I knew the rest of the story would have to wait.

+ +

Archie's neighbors, Arlene and Edell, assumed that a healthy twenty-seven-year old man would soon recover from the virus. However, they doubted Lorene would care for her husband properly and tried to help as best they could. Arlene stopped by once or twice a week to check with Lorene on things, bringing food but limiting her contact time. No one wanted that bug. One day, toward the end of Archie's illness, Arlene knocked on his door.

"Who's there?" It was little Charles' voice from behind the closed door.

"It's me, Mrs. Ware. Just wanted to see how your father's doing."

"Ma's not home." The boy opened the door. Arlene was shocked at how emaciated he looked.

"I brought you some soup. There should be enough for everyone. Let me put it in the kitchen. Your momma can reheat it. When's she coming back?" Arlene stepped into the living room and headed for the kitchen.

"I don't know." As he said this, his two sisters poked their heads in from the hallway.

"How long has she been gone?" Arlene asked, masking her shock and horror as she observed the children's gauntness.

"Two days."

"Two days!" Arlene said, unable to hide her surprise. A look of disgust followed. "Who's staying with you kids?"

"No one. Ma never lets no one stay with us, except sometimes when one of our uncles sleeps late, and she has to leave."

"So, no one stays with you kids when she's gone? No one's here to look after the three of you?"

"I do. Ma always tells me to look after myself and Shirley and Betty."

Arlene looked at the small boy, then continued on into the kitchen and sat the crock of soup down on the kitchen counter. She found this maneuver somewhat difficult as dirty dishes and pots were strewn everywhere on the counter, as well as on a small table in the room.

The sink was also piled high with dirty dishes. Archie had been sick for almost a month. She turned and looked at his son.

“Why did your mother leave? Was there some sort of emergency?”

“I dunno. She leaves every couple of days.”

“The whole time since your daddy became sick?”

“Yessum.”

Arlene walked down the hallway to Archie’s bedroom. She cracked the door, peaked in, and was horrified. He lay on the bed, softly moaning, a shell of his former masculine self. She closed the door and walked back to the living room.

“Little Charles, stay here. I’m getting a doctor.” She could not help thinking how emaciated the children looked as she hurried out of the front door. By the time a doctor looked at Archie, it was too late to reverse his condition. Lorene returned later that day and feigned surprise at her husband’s condition. She promised to stay with him thereafter. His death the second week of October shocked no one.

Afterward, Lorene complained to her mother-in-law, “I ain’t got no money for no funeral.”

+ +

“So, my Red Headed Granny killed granddaddy?”

"That's never been proven, just suspected. Most of the town thought she purposefully neglected him, even denied him care and medicines that might have helped him. He was a strong, healthy young man, and they had the best chance of surviving the flu."

"If that's true, how could Daddy have even let her in this house two years ago?"

"That's a good question. All I know is that your father is a one in a million. Nobody else like him."

"Who paid for Granddaddy's funeral?"

"Who do you think? His mother."

\+ \+

Several days after the funeral, Lorene sat little Charles and his two sisters down and explained how things would be going forward.

"Your daddy is dead now, so you're going to have to look after yourselves more. I got to earn a living, so I ain't going to be here all the time. You girls are going to have to do what your brother says, and Charles, you're going to have to start pulling your own weight around here more."

For Charles, pulling his own weight brought more changes, all for the worse. Lorene's presence became rarer as she took a job at a diner in a nearby town. She also increased her sleepovers with boyfriends who lived there. Charles continued to feed himself and his sisters as he had during his father's illness, only with less food available. He had stopped going to school shortly after his father became ill in order to look after his sisters. Going back now was out of question as he had to shine shoes downtown for grocery money. He resorted to begging, but this left him feeling ashamed. All three children experienced constant hunger and lost more weight.

Arlene dropped by one day and asked, "Your momma out again?"

"Yessum. She's workin' at the diner."

"Well, I made more than we can eat, so here's some leftovers. I'll come by tomorrow and get the dishes back." Walking away, she wondered how the three kids managed to survive.

Both Archie and Lorene came from large families. Several of the kid's relatives decided to take Betty and Shirley. In mid-January, each went to live with a different aunt while Charles remained in the house, alone. Splitting the sisters up and separating them from their brother devastated the trio, but they had no choice. Lorene did not notice the girls were gone until one night in early February.

"Where's your sisters? I told you to look after them! Have you let them go somewheres outside?"

"Ma…" Charles hesitated to speak, knowing his mother's temper could result in a beating. "They been gone since last month."

"What're you talking about?! Whadda you mean they been gone?!"

"Aunt Mamie took Shirley, and Aunt Elsie took Betty. They been living with them since December."

"Why didn't you tell me?! I can't trust you to take care of things, can I?!"

Charles was too scared to tell her he had tried to let her know about the girls the few times she was home. Either tired, drunk, or with a man, Lorene was in no condition or mood to understand. Despite her anger at learning this had happened without her knowledge, Charles perceived that his mother was actually happy at the news.

After this episode, Charles' heartbreak increased. Lorene came home more frequently as she no longer had to sneak men in after the kids were asleep. A routine developed that Charles remembered the rest of his life. Several nights a week, Lorene would come home from work, usually around 6 pm, with a man, often someone Charles had never met before. Introductions followed a pattern.

"Charles, say 'hey' to your Uncle Bob," Lorene commanded. If Charles failed to respond promptly or properly, Lorene scolded, "Are you an idiot? Don't you know how to say 'hey'?"

"Hey Uncle Bob."

"Hey Charles."

Cruelest part of the routine, she next took her little son's hand and guided him to the door that led down to the basement. If he began crying en route, she whipped him with one hand while dragging him with the other. She next deposited him at the top of the basement stairs, then shut the door. Charles always remembered the cruel click as she locked it. He spent most nights in the basement in February, March, and April, cold and scared in a dark world.

"Ma, please let me out!" Sobs and crying accompanied his pleas to her.

Sometimes, he heard no response, other times, he heard threats.

"Shut up, or I'll come down there, and you'll be sorry."

At first that quieted Charles, but eventually he longed for anything that opened the basement door and let in light.

"Ma, please! Please!"

When enough of his pleas opened the door, beatings followed, sometimes from one of his 'uncles.' He suffered in darkness. Some nights, the laughter and lewd sounds above were the only things that provided any awareness that life existed outside that basement. He always remained there until his 'uncle' left in the morning.

In early May, Lorene made an announcement.

"I'm gonna be leaving for a while. I got an opportunity up in Indiana that I need to look into."

"What are you gonna do? Who'll look after me? Don't you love me anymore?"

"You're gonna be okay. You been lookin' after yourself pretty good anyways. Arlene and Edell will keep an eye on you."

"What about Shirley and Betty?"

"What about 'em? Their aunts are taking care of them."

Lorene left that evening, despite Charles' sobs. She walked out of the house and hopped into a truck passing through, driven by a truck driver she met at the diner earlier that day. From the front porch, Charles watched her drive off, never to return other than for an extremely rare visit. The seven-year old stood all alone but was at least not locked in the basement.

Things didn't change much for Charles after his mother left. He had previously looked after himself and his sisters for many months. Now, he only had to look after himself.

\+ +

I looked at Momma in amazement after she paused in her story. She shook her head as she said, "Unbelievable, if it wasn't true."

"I never knew that about Daddy. So, that's why he always wants the light left on."

"Yes. He can't stand total darkness after all the nights he spent locked in that dark basement. That woman never even left any sort of a light on for him down there."

"Why?! Why would she do that?"

"Who knows? Cruelty? Thoughtlessness? No, she did think about herself… only herself. I never liked being around her, even though I only saw her twice after we married. She didn't even bother to come to our wedding."

"How could Daddy even allow her in the house two years ago? I'd have kicked her out."

"I wanted to. Your daddy is a remarkable man."

"So, what happened after the Red Headed Granny left for Indiana?"

"Some of it you already know. When he turned eighteen, your daddy enlisted in the Navy. Before that, he was completely on his own. He looked after himself. Lorene sent rent checks to the landlord a couple of months, then stopped. The landlord was surprised when he came to collect overdue rent to find that only your father was living in the house. The landlord arranged for him to live with the Wares for a short while. Then, your daddy pretty much led a nomadic existence, moving in temporarily with a relative or neighbor, then leaving after a month or two. This was during the Depression, and everyone was poor. Homeless children were everywhere, and another mouth to feed was a big burden. Sometimes he lived on the street, slept in vacant buildings, scrounged for food. He existed like this for eleven years until he joined the Navy. After the Navy, he married me and worked hard to make a good life for his family."

So angry at my Red Headed Granny, I could find no words and simply nodded.

"It's always been tough for him to think about those days. For years after we got married, he'd wake up once or twice a month in the middle of the night from nightmares. Our bed sheets would be soaked with his sweat." Momma shook her head in sympathy."I tried to get him to tell me about it, but he wouldn't talk. I had to pry it out of him that the nightmares were about being alone in the dark in his mom's basement. Eventually, he told me about his mother and her carryings-on."

"I'm amazed he didn't get into crime or drugs."

"Yeah… It kind of goes against what most people would expect. Your daddy has a lot of strength of character."

"What about Aunt Shirley and Aunt Betty?"

"They got passed around by relatives pretty much until they turned eighteen. Each girl stayed with someone for six, maybe twelve months, then got passed to another. Betty did wind up in an orphanage for about five years."

"Why didn't any of the relatives take in Daddy?"

"No one wanted a young boy. Especially when he became a teenager. They figured he would be in too much trouble."

Anger and hatred stirred in me. I said, "What a tramp! I still don't understand why Daddy even allowed her in this house."

"Your daddy is like a lot of children with bad parents. I've seen it with children of alcoholics. They can't reject the person who gave them life. Something inside them makes them want to keep some sort of bond with their parents, even though that person neglected and abused them."

"That Red Headed Granny kept him locked in a cold, dark basement while she slept with other men." Now, I shook my head. "No wonder he always keeps a light on when he sleeps."

"Yep. That's why."

I racked my brain. How could a wife deliberately engineer the homicide of her husband? How could a mother abandon her three young children? Was she some sort of homicidal psychopath? She must be the closest living thing to pure evil that ever touched my life.

"She better not ever come here again. I'll tear her apart."

+ +

I meant every word, but fifty-one years later, I know better. Time gives a person perspective. Aunt Betty and Aunt Shirley got married, had children, and lived happily until they passed away in their seventies. Fond memories of them visiting us sometimes surface in my lagging memory.

Lorene led a sad life after she left Archie. She went through a succession of husbands and eventually passed away. I heard that only three people were at her funeral, one of them being the undertaker and none of them family.

Daddy joined the Navy, got married, and raised a good family. Just before he died in 1977, I asked him how he had found it in his heart to forgive a mother who abandoned him. His words, “Lorene probably did the best thing she could do for me when she left me,” still echo.

After he died, I thought of something else I wished I had asked. Was her leaving best because it freed him from her and her bad influence? Or because in her own way, it was the most she was able to do for him? Either way, he died without malice toward his mother, which was the best thing he could do.

The night Momma watched Tom Jones sing on Johnny Carson however, malice stewed within me. Momma wisely let me simmer without argument. She simply stood and beckoned me to go to bed.

\+ \+

“Mom… you okay?” my Gen Z daughter asked. “For a minute, you looked like you were tripping out on me.”

I smiled. “No, just thinking. What was it you said?”

“Don’t turn out the light.”

LIQUOR BOY

When Longfellow said "Into each life some rain must fall" in his poem The Rainy Day, he must have been thinking about the Liquor Boy.

He began his sad, poignant story over glasses of Hess Chardonnay while he and I sat in the Bistro at Persnickety's. We nicknamed him 'the Liquor Boy' shortly after he replaced 'the Liquor Man' about two years ago. Neither of them re-stocked hard liquor at Persnickety's. Grocery stores in Alabama can only sell beer and wine, and both of those working stiffs only handled the wine part. Alabama ABC laws are almost as out of date as those in Pennsylvania. I know. I lived there three miserable years. Despite this kind of legal nonsense, somehow Liquor instead of Wine became part of the unofficial titles given them by Persnickety's customers.

The Liquor Boy reminded me of a nineteen-year-old Elvis Presley—same long wavy black hair, flawless youthful skin that never knew a smear of Clearasil, blue eyes reminiscent of one of my favorite flowers, forget-me-nots. His "yes ma'am" and "thanka vury much" unintentionally mimicked that of 'The King'. Had I been twenty years younger and single, he could have slept in my bed any night. And the 'single' part could have easily been ignored had it not been applicable. That day, I settled for wine and conversation delving into man's inhumanity to man and ways government abets that cruelty.

"Y'all seem a little down today," I said, revealing the reason I invited him to join me at one of three tables in what passes at

Persnickety's for a bistro. "Maybe a little wine will improve your karma."

"Yes ma'am. It's been pretty rough today," Liquor Boy said.

He had finished re-stocking the woefully inadequate alcove set aside in Persnickety's for wine and was on his way out when I noticed he seemed out of kilter. Not his usual youthful 'I'm not worried about Social Security going broke because I'll fund my retirement on my own' outlook on life. I was squeezing lemons in the fruits and veggies section when he drag-assed his way past me without even a "Hey" to acknowledge my existence. My motherly instinct kicked in. I intentionally pushed my grocery cart into his hand truck and said, "Okay, out with it. Tell momma. What's your problem?"

"I'm quittin'. I just cain't take it anymore."

Persnickety's was the most upscale of three grocery stores on his route in our small Alabama town. He delivered a variety of wines there on Mondays and Thursdays. All the ladies, myself included, eagerly anticipated an eye candy feast on those days. Sensual dance-like maneuvering of his hand truck preceded chest and arm muscles flexing as he unboxed and positioned his wares on shelves. Competition for the limited selection of wines that resulted from his efforts also fueled our anticipation. Why is it limited? Liquor, beer, and wine sales are rigidly controlled by an Alcoholic Beverage Control

(ABC) Board in our state. The Liquor Boy's woes largely flowed from that entity.

I had flirted with him enough over the past two years that I knew he would be susceptible to a glass of wine or two. I immediately invited him over to the Bistro for a little sympathy. Persnickety's was always the last stop on his route, so I knew he would have time to spend with me before returning to the awful ochre-colored metal building behind the Coca-Cola bottling plant that passes for an ABC Store.

After I ordered our wine and we sat down, I asked, "What happened to make you want to quit?"

"I ran out of Kenwood."

"Why am I not surprised?! I saw Persnickety's half-off ads on Kenwood in the paper yesterday." I made no attempt to hide my disgust. "It's ridiculous that this state's ABC Board determines how much wine and liquor each store is allotted. Them ABC bureaucrats never give y'all enough of whatever the stores advertise."

"Yes ma'am. ABC didn't allot nearly enough to cover Kroger, Publix, and Persnickety's. People at Publix were fightin' each other over what little Kenwood I had left after Kroger. There weren't none left for Persnickety's."

It reminded me of the fights we used to have over Snackwell's Devil's Food cookies when they came out in 1992. All the moms would cluster around the endcap in Kroger, waiting to pounce when the Nabisco Man made his delivery.

"I can imagine what happened. They took it out on you." I nodded in sympathy, knowing how shoppers, especially those pursuing wine, can be vicious.

"Yes ma'am. I thought Miss Bevis and Miss Singletary was gonna hit me. I tried tellin' 'em it weren't my fault. I cain't help what them ABC people give me."

"More importantly, what they don't give you."

"Yes ma'am… I just cain't take it no more." His head slumped. I could not help but ogle that head full of beautiful black hair and mentally chastised myself for lusting during his time of woe.

"I know it's been two years of hell for you, but you can't quit. You've been doing a great job. Much better than… than…" I could not even remember the Liquor Man's actual name. I did remember that he often suffered similar bouts of depression at having to deal with irate customers as well as the ABC Board. How he had lasted so long is anyone's guess. "Everyone knows it's not your fault these grocery stores don't have enough wine."

Still looking down, he said, "It's not just that they don't have enough, they also limit the different brands we can distribute. Miss Melson has been asking Publix to stock Barboursville for months, and they still don't have it. I think she blames me."

Our ABC Board has regulations that it conveniently uses to limit selection. Pity poured forth from my mouth.

"Bless your soul. I know it's rough. I know."

"Y'all don't know the half of it, ma'am… y'all jus' don't know…" His voice trailed off. He lifted his head, and those gorgeous blue eyes looked up into mine. I could feel my resistance weakening but willed myself not to think carnal thoughts as a single tear rolled down his cheek.

"Tell Momma. Maybe I can help." I took his hands in mine.

"Used to be it was never enough Petite Syrah. Them women used to follow me down the aisle complainin' about Kroger always being out of Petite Syrah, so I complain and complain, and finally them ABC folks increase my allotment. Just when I'm gettin' my shelves lookin' pretty good with Petite Syrah, all of a sudden, dry Rosé catches on. Mister Oakley starts harpin' about dry Rosé. When I asked them ABC folks to start stockin' it, they don't even know what dry Rosé is. I try telling Miss Betterton that it ain't me, and she says that I ain't assertive enough… that I outta be more of a man and make them ABC folks stock dry Rosé."

"Don't listen to her," I soothed. "Agnes Betterton is a Humira-popping manic depressive. Everyone knows you are doing your best to get folks the wines they want."

"It's not just that. It's a lot of other stuff as well."

It sounded like this might be worse than I had initially suspected. A poor wine selection is bad enough. Pile other alcoholic issues on top, and I could understand how an impressionable young man might become seriously depressed.

"What do you mean?" I asked.

"I mean like… what do I know about screw-top versus corked bottles? Why do folks constantly ask me about that? I don't know which is best. They all taste pretty good to me. But these women, they either hate screw top or they wish all wine bottles was screw top. They act as if I had a choice and brung in the vury ones they don't like on purpose…"

I slowly shook my head in sympathy. He lowered his head again before continuing, "And them composite corks! Everyone hates them things. Everyone complains to me about them… they won't come out… they disintegrate… they's too ugly to make trivets with 'em. Like it's all my fault…"

His voice trailed off. A moment of silence ensued during which I vainly searched for some words of comfort. All I could manage to say was something everyone says when they don't know what to say. "Is there anything I can do to help?"

"No ma'am. I've had enough of this job. I cain't even rip open the top of a wine box without them women grabbing the bottles before I can put 'em on the shelf. And Miss Pettus always grabs more than her share. The other women complain to me about it. They say I should limit how many she can have. That ain't my responsibility, is it?" he pleaded.

"No, it ain't. It's the store manager's," I replied. Beverly Pettus' greed was widely known throughout Persnickety's, but I had never despised her for it as much as I did then. I finished my glass of Chardonnay and headed for the counter. "Let me get us another round."

"Thanka vury much."

My hands held two glasses of a cheap Pinot Grigio as I returned. He sat with his head in his hands and did not even look up as I placed a glass in front of him. All I could think of was that I had paid more for two glasses of this stuff than I would have for a whole bottle of the high-end stuff they sell at Dollar General. Trembling in his voice brought me back.

"How… how… how in the heck do I know what kind of corkscrew is best? Seems to me, it's a matter of personal preference. Some people likes winged corkscrews, some people likes plain ole twist corkscrews. Don't ever get between Miss Bobo and Miss Sheffield when they's arguin' about corkscrews 'cause one of 'em is gonna take it out on y'all when y'all say y'all favor what she don't like."

"I know sweetie. I've been there."

"And them notes…"

Quickly redirecting my gaze downward, I felt my face flush crimson as I suspected the subject of his next gripe.

"They leave them little notes for me on the shelves." His face contorted with emotion as he related example contents from several notes. "When are y'all gonna get more Cabernet in? How come y'all never stock a decent Pinot Noir? I'm gonna start buying all my wine in Mississippi. Most of them notes don't even have a signature on 'em."

I fidgeted and focused on my nails, being one of those leaving him little notes. I finally said, "You gotta learn to let that stuff roll off your back… like water off a duck's. Just ignore the notes. They don't mean anything… most of 'em anyway."

"It's hard to ignore 'em, Ma'am. Some of 'em make naughty proposals."

He told me nothing I did not already know. We called them 'Liquor Boy Love Notes.' I decided to change the subject.

"Maybe you need a vacation. Why don't you take a long weekend and go to Gulf Shores?"

"It'd jus' be the same bullsh…" He caught himself. "The same stuff when I get back. No ma'am. I'm quittin'. I cain't take all them irate customers and them stupid ABC folks anymore."

I nodded, remembering an incident the Liquor Man and I had with the ABC Board years ago. There was a nice wine I had asked him to stock. Problem was the label on the bottle had a sketch of a nude woman on it. I think it was a copy of a Cézanne. The Liquor Man requested the ABC Board stock it, but they refused, explaining that the sketch was indecent. Ironically, I subsequently had him ask, and they approved, stocking a Ménage à Trois red blend. We both laughed our asses off over the fact that those ABC idiots obviously did not speak French.

Again, I took his hands in mine to comfort him. My fingertips felt the smooth, soft flesh on the backs of his hands and how it contrasted with the rough calluses on his palms. My thoughts again strayed. Stumbling for words, I muttered, "Sometimes I wonder if those people at the ABC have got the brains God gave a billy goat."

"Yes ma'am." The Liquor Boy nodded. "It's like them wine bags. All the grocery stores want to offer 'em as a bagging option. Y'all know… to help reduce plastic and cardboard waste. Folks like 'em, 'specially when they got cool logos or funny cartoons on 'em. But the ABC Board won't allow stores to offer 'em as an option to bag y'all's wine in. I just wish someone could explain that to me."

"Yeah. When you got three or four bottles, you don' need a big cardboard box, and trying to haul that many to your car in plastic bags is a hassle for sure. That's why I bring my own wine bags."

"I bet more folks would use 'em, but not many knows about 'em since ABC prevents stores from offering 'em."

I thought, *Once again, government regulators are reducing our options, acting like little dictators on high. No wonder he wants out.*

"I'm gettin' tired of trying to sneak in with my deliveries. I cain't go in any grocery store, even when I'm just shoppin' for myself, without a bunch of women chasin' me down the aisles, asking 'bout a Beaulieu Merlot or an Oak Ridge Zinfandel…"

As he said the word 'chasing', I wondered if those women were using their wine questions merely as a pretext to get into his pants. I let that thought drop.

"Can I ask y'all something?" he asked.

My ears perked up. I won't say what I hoped he was going to ask.

"Sure. Anything y'all want to ask. Go ahead. I'm ready."

"What's a Chablis? Miss Isbell asked me this morning why we don't stock it. I felt kinda stupid. I didn't tell her that I'd never heard of it. I just stood there lookin' stupid. Sounds French. Y'all think it's a French wine?"

Chabis?! I thought to myself, *Such an innocent child!* His impressive intellect often makes us forget his youth. It was only two months ago that a bunch of us brought strawberry cupcakes with sprinkles on them to celebrate his twenty-third birthday. No one his age could possibly know what Chablis is because stores seldom stock it anymore. The wine one drinks only when one has to. I quit drinking Chablis after my husband became a director in the early 1990s. Immediately after this thought, memories of Chablis with squirt cheese on Triscuits sent shivers down my spine.

"Sweetie, it's just a cheap American wine. Only a fool like Liz Isbell would be asking for something that nobody drinks anymore."

"She called me a buffoon... a hick... said I was nowheres near the liquor man that my predecessor was..."

Liz Isbell was lucky she was not there, or I would have pulled her blonde hair out by its dark roots.

"She said I should probably find a line of work more suited to me..." Lines of anger creased his forehead as he related that woman's cruelty. "When she said it, she pointed over to the vegetable department. I knew what she meant."

"You cain't let one ole bitch get you down. No one's been better at keeping Persnickety's wine department stocked than you. Some women are going to complain about something just so's they can complain. Don't take it seriously. It's nothing."

"Yes, it is. It's serious. The Kroger manager's always harping on me about all the rain checks he's having to give out on my wines. These women all blame me for not having the wine that's advertised in Tuesday's paper. Miss Woodis even threatened to write the Governor about it."

I was surprised she did not threaten to write to the President. The woman has nothing better to do other than write letters to Dear Abby. I tried to change the subject. "What do you think about stemless wine glasses? I'm on the fence myself."

"Miss Kirkland was talking to me about that yesterday at Publix. She said the old traditional glasses with stems don't fit in her new dishwasher. Too much stem, too little bowl."

He held up his glass to the light, admired it, and took a long pull. When he finished, he put the glass down on the table and said something so profound that I will never forget it.

"I bet they took them stems off because they finally realized people have enough fingers to hold a stemless glass."

It took me a while to comprehend the meaning of his observation. A person can hold a stemmed wine glass using one finger and a thumb, something tough to do with a stemless wine glass. A full minute of speechless silence passed before I could respond.

"I don't think I've ever heard anyone say something so wise. I wish you would reconsider quitting. We will sorely miss your wisdom."

In a display of determination, he shook his head, causing his long thick black hair to sway erotically.

"No ma'am. I'm gonna quit. This wine business is too tough. I cain't take it anymore. I've got to find something less stressful. My momma's been tellin' me to find another job. Says nothing's worth this kind of pain. Says I could do better for myself. My momma's pretty smart."

"What momma ain't?" I agreed. Obviously, he was serious. I could not imagine anyone else doing his job as well as he did. No more eye candy. I held back my tears and tried to look optimistic for his sake. "What will you do? You got anything in mind?"

"Yes ma'am. I've already talked to someone, and he said one of his employees is retiring. Said the job's mine, if I want it. I start in two weeks."

My philosophy has always been that all jobs are the same. After your first six months honeymoon, you pretty much hate whatever you're doing. It follows that if you're going to hate any job in the long run, why not take the job that pays the most money?

"I hope you'll get a nice raise. What job is it?"

Pride burst forth from his countenance. He beamed.

"I'll be taking over the Budweiser Man's route."

OLD FRIENDS

Old friends turn
up in the
strangest
places.

Why?

Life is full of
confusion.
Confusion of
love, passion,
and romance.

~Matthew
Underwood

Unrequited love
differs from
mutual love, just
like delusion
differs from the
truth.

~George Sand

Fog

Ethereal fog wafted in the darkness of a place Amelia seldom visited, until lately. At this late hour, she normally slept peacefully in her college dorm room. This night was different, as it had been for many nights recently. Tonight, she walked along streets blanketed with cloudy mist. She detected no reason for her subliminal stroll, other than it was beyond her control. Amelia's life had been like this for weeks—going through the motions, living in a fog, and not knowing why things happened the way they did.

Tonight's fog seemed to differ from the kind typically occurring this time of year. It was not the thick heavy stuff weighed down with springtime moisture and pollen. That fog stands still and makes you push your way through it. You have to know what you're doing and where you're going in order to get where you want to go. This light airy stuff seemed to float and bounce about randomly, yielding no clue as to which way to go. It mirrored her current state of mind.

Scary movies love fog. It enhances a sense of foreboding. Moviegoers never know what or when something bad is going to pop out on the screen. They only know that something bad is happening, and that something worse is going to happen. Amelia felt that way tonight. She suspected worse things were coming.

Woe burdened Amelia. She felt dull, foolish, confused, in sync with the cloudy disorientation caused by this fog. No wonder they cite the 'fog of war' as descriptive of the confusion that occurs in battle. Amelia's confusion resulted from ignorance. She did not understand the reasons behind the cause of her misery. Finding her way out of this stuff seemed impossible. She suddenly remembered a quote from one of her favorite paranormal romance novels. "You never realized how thick your fog was until it lifted," [J.R. Ward, *Lover Reborn*]. That thought triggered others.

I don't see any street signs? How do I know which way to turn? I might as well be in a corn maze.

Amelia had wandered through each day adrift, not knowing which way to turn, just as she did now. She wanted to know why these things had happened to her, but no answer came. Ignorance reigned, and one of its offspring, depression, set in. Although she told no one, she questioned whether life itself was worth living. Now, she numbly felt street pavement beneath her feet and could do nothing except move toward something, anything.

In unrestful moments before her midnight strolls, Amelia would lay in her dorm room bed and look up. A face repeated itself in some of the swirls in her stucco ceiling. She also heard the face's voice echoing in night sounds outside her window. Tears always accompanied these sleepless nights, but Amelia's yielded no relief as tears sometimes do.

Her days were no better than her nights. Some mornings, Amelia couldn't decide whether to stay in bed or get up. Invariably, she stayed in bed. The mornings she did get up, she went to class depressed and in a daze. She sat in class, her mind uncontrollably drifting to the cause of her pain. Assignments went undone. Instructors took note of behavior uncharacteristic of a senior English honors student. Her advisor suggested a visit to the college's medical clinic where they found nothing physically wrong.

The same question haunted Amelia night and day, asleep and awake.

Why, why, why?

Tonight's fog provided no answer. Neither did Amelia's parents provide an answer, especially her father. He believed the cause of her pain, not uncommon among young women her age, to be easily remedied. She resented it when he attempted to cheer her up by making light of it.

Those her own age empathized with Amelia's plight, her roommate being one of these. Her efforts to console Amelia failed. Tonight, her roommate slept peacefully, unaware of Amelia's nocturnal wandering.

As she stumbled along, another quote, this one from one of her favorite poets, came to mind, "Love is kind of like when you see a fog in the morning, when you wake up before the sun comes out. It's just a little while, and then it burns away… with the first daylight of reality," [Charles Bukowski].

How true, Amelia thought as she ambled forward, how true.

Old Friend in a Bar

It materialized amongst the mist as if by magic. Gilded letters formed the words, 'KING'S TAVERN', stenciled on a window that flanked a solid mahogany door accessing a stately old building. Relief began to flood Amelia much as a spring rain brings life to struggling seeds.

This might be a place she could get information on where she was and directions where to go. The building itself offered reassurance. Gracefully aged with hand-cut sandstone that must have been set in place by a master builder long ago, it reminded Amelia of many buildings on her own college campus. For over three years, that campus offered her comfort as she acquired knowledge. The mahogany wood of the door glowed with a rich patina that bespoke many years of providing an entrance into the building. She excitedly directed her steps straight for the door.

Once at the doorstep, Amelia extended one hand and grasped the doorknob. She pulled while twisting at the same time but was surprised at how it resisted opening. She extended her other hand, placed it on top of the other that still held the doorknob within its grip, and pulled a second time, this time applying more force. With effort, the door opened. She stepped inside, not knowing exactly why she was drawn into this particular establishment, other than the relief it seemed to offer from darkness and fog that beset her during her nighttime wandering. I knew why.

I knew the establishment's cozy intimacy, buttressed by walnut paneled walls and plush deep purple leather chairs would calm her agitated mind. I knew the classic hunt prints adorning the walls would remind her of good times at her parents' house. An excellent copy of one of them, 'The Master and Hounds', still hung in her father's study. I knew reminiscences of agreeable things tend to ease a troubled mind.

Amelia stood quietly and took in the building's interior. A luxurious dark walnut stain highlighted the paneling's fine wood grain. Its satin wood grain was enhanced by light given off from the polished brass light fixtures. A polished mahogany bar glowed and its brass rail gleamed as if it had been 'spit-shined.' She marveled not only at the room's elegance, but at how everything had been chosen with care and seemed to be in perfect placement. Obviously, a topnotch designer had a hand in such work. Her desire to receive the relief offered inside, instead of returning outside to the fog, increased.

"Amelia, my pet. Over here."

The husky voice with an ever-so-slight Scottish accent emanated from a distinguished looking figure sitting at a two-top against a wall opposite the bar. She turned to see an old and very close friend last seen three months ago when she went home for Christmas vacation. Amelia remembered her vacation with bitter-sweetness, as the end of her happy times. The last of the 'good ole days' when things were brighter. She longed to turn the clock back to those days when her mind understood things better. She wished she had spent more time with her old friend during Christmas vacation.

With a movement of his head, Rex again beckoned her. Watching her approach, he appraised her appearance. Physically, she appeared little changed. Tall, not nearly as towheaded as when he first met her thirteen years ago, seductive green eyes, and a smile that said, 'You're still my best friend.' A reciprocal smile spread across Rex' face.

Amelia always loved Rex's smile. It never failed to materialize whenever she came into his presence. She knew it to be heartfelt, indicative of the love and devotion he felt for her, and equal to that which she felt for him. Although he was now much older than Amelia, they still possessed a close bond.

It formed the first moment they met over thirteen years ago when he moved into her neighborhood. I knew Rex' personality significantly contributed to that bond. Several of his personality traits come to mind, reserved but affectionate being foremost. He limited his circle of friends to a select few, but for those so selected, he lavished them with a close, personal love. Gentle also comes to mind when describing Rex. Unlike other older males in her neighborhood, Rex treated Amelia and her playmates gently, never complaining when their loud noise and hectic playtime reached obnoxious levels.

Other notable characteristics? Brave and protective. I knew Amelia's parents subconsciously relaxed more if they saw Rex taking it easy on his front porch while their daughter played in their front yard. Several times he raced from his perch into their yard to prevent the youngster from carelessly wandering into the path of an oncoming car. From Amelia's perspective, Rex's most valiant effort occurred the time he intervened to protect her from a stray poisonous snake, a story she often retold.

In route to Rex's table, she noted a few new strands of grey amongst that already populating the thick, auburn mane luxuriously covering the top of her old friend's head. Next to this, she had always thought his nose to be one of his most distinguishing features. Long and straight, she wondered why that shape was called a Greek nose. She also remembered hearing that a Greek nose indicates intelligence, certainly true in his case. His nose separated two beautiful, almond-shaped brown eyes. Everything visually reinforced a countenance bespeaking sophistication and wisdom. Rex appeared much like his normal self. Other than something he wore.

"I love your smoking jacket. I've never seen you in one before," Amelia said upon arriving at his table.

The wine-colored, silken velvet jacket seemed to be complemented by the deep purple color of the leather chair in which he sat. Rex reminded Amelia of the old movies from the thirties that starred William Powell. The actor sometimes wore a smoking jacket and stood next to a fancy silver bar cart as he prepared martinis. The epitome of sophistication and wisdom. Smartest person in the room, Nick Charles always answered the 'whodunit' question by the end of the movie.

That jacket fits his personality to a tee, she thought. *Why couldn't other males be more like Rex? Smart. Sophisticated. Unselfish. Loving. Faithful.*

"Thank you. It's a Turnbull & Asser. I wore it to the opera before I came here. Won't you join me?"

Amelia thought, *A smoking jacket at the opera? At a bar?*

As if reading her mind, Rex said, "My dear, depending on style, smoking jackets are appropriate at black tie affairs, including the opera and most certainly in a bar meeting someone as treasured as you."

Rex's complement sent a dose of elation straight into Amelia's heart, the first in weeks. She wanted to pirouette on her tiptoes and shout with joy in response. She also wanted to affect a level of sophistication in front of her old friend and instead, asked a question, "What opera did you see?"

"Puccini's *Madame Butterfly*."

"Ooh! I've heard of that opera all my life but have never seen it. How was it? What's it about?"

The smile on Rex's face turned to a frown which Amelia interpreted as his attempt to be melodramatic.

"Oh, my friend, it's a sad story about unrequited love. A young Japanese geisha falls in love with an American Naval officer. He uses her, then returns to America. While he is away, the geisha has his child. The officer returns to Japan… with his American wife. There is a lot of drama and music before the geisha commits suicide in the end. You must see it one day."

During Rex's synopsis, Amelia had paused mid-flight in her effort to sit down. Rex noted this and said, "Please, please…sit down. We need to catch up."

As she finished sitting down, I could read Amelia's mind. *It is truly a shame that more males aren't like Rex. He still looks good. Hasn't aged much over the years.*

Rex was in his late fifties when she started college over three years ago. He still lived in Amelia's hometown, and they now saw each other only on holiday and vacation breaks. I knew Rex was disappointed during her last Christmas vacation, as much of her time was spent with her boyfriend, Dylan. Dylan lived in another town, so Amelia cut short time spent at her parents' house in order to visit him.

Rex remembered watching her pack her car the afternoon of Christmas Day and being sad when she drove off. She had mentioned to him the day before that she was going to spend the rest of her vacation with Dylan and hopefully would be able to spend a little more time with Rex on her spring break.

Thoughts of Dylan stirred painful emotions in Amelia. Sensing this, Rex said, "Talk to me."

"You always know what I'm thinking, don't you?"

Rex nodded, first at Amelia, then at the bartender. He said, "I must apologize. I forgot to ask if you want something to drink. Do you still like Cosmopolitans? I remember that was the first drink you ordered on your twenty-first birthday last October."

Amelia nodded acceptance and smiled at both his thoughtfulness and accent. She thought the 'ah' sound when he said 'ask' was priceless. Rex relayed their orders to the bartender as the older gentleman approached.

"A Cosmopolitan for the young lady, please, and another Macallan for me."

After he departed, Amelia said, "You still know what I like. It's like you've always been my alter ego..." Unable to finish her thoughts, Amelia's eyes dropped.

"You were going to add, 'unlike Dylan', weren't you?"

"Yes."

Rex allowed her a period of silence to collect her thoughts. While waiting, he thought back to the first time he had met Dylan. It was the summer break after Amelia's sophomore year in college. They were both students at the same college, and Dylan drove over to spend the Fourth of July holiday with her. Rex remembered getting bad vibes from the start. The kid was tall, even taller than Amelia, and skinny as a beanpole. Despite it being the middle of summer, he looked as white as a bedsheet. Rex took one look at Dylan's hair and wanted to run away.

He remembered the comment Amelia's father made to him afterward. He said, "Looks like this kid shaved the sides and back of his head, then stuck the top of his head in a blender." Rex later found out that Dylan's haircut was called a Spiked Hair plus High Skin Fade.

Rex asked himself, *Good Lord! Who thought that one up?*

Amelia introduced Dylan to Rex, and although Rex sensed the young man was not deserving of Amelia, he nevertheless put on his best friendly act. It did not matter as it was obvious that Dylan had little time for an old friend of Amelia's. Rex thought his behavior to be revealing, much less than expected of someone who is truly honest and caring.

He remembered Dylan's sarcastic commit, "You're not looking too bad for such an old guy." From the first moment Rex met him, he sensed Dylan cared for no one but himself. Nothing since then had changed his mind. Rex's mind returned to the present and Amelia.

Sensing she might be ready to talk, Rex asked, "Do you feel like talking about it? It might help. It always did. Remember?"

His words jogged old memories. Amelia remembered sitting together on the front porch swing, telling Rex all her innermost secrets. Rex knew when to speak, but more importantly, he instinctively knew when to be silent and simply listen. Amelia always did all the talking. No wonder her nickname was 'Miss Motormouth'. Some weekends they sat like that for hours, Rex listening, like an old friend was supposed to. He never interrupted, instead allowing her to vent her frustrations, express her aspirations, and tell him things she would never tell anyone else. Amelia knew her secrets would be safe with Rex.

That was perhaps the thing she missed most in college. Amelia enjoyed her roommates. She was on her fourth roommate as she had a new roommate every year. You could talk with them, and she did all the time. But it wasn't the same as talking to Rex. They didn't listen as well as he did. There were some things you couldn't tell them because you knew they would think badly of you or worse, get texted all over campus. Rex was different. There was nothing you couldn't tell him. Rex was never judgmental, and what you told him stayed with him and him alone. He always seemed to understand when you told him what you had done or what you were thinking. It was so nice to have an old friend like Rex. Amelia thought about this, looked at Rex, and nodded affirmatively to his question.

"Why…" Amelia paused as several tears crawled down her cheeks. She wiped them away, tried to continue, but could not. Rex wisely said nothing, letting her emotions take their course. Shortly, she collected herself, sighed deeply, and asked one question, "Why don't people you love, love you back?"

An age-old question, thought and asked by lovers and writers everywhere. Who knows the answer to that question? The answer might have alleviated untold heartache. It might permit people throughout the world to know the contentment that comes from understanding the answer.

"I wish I knew the answer to that," Rex subtly, but wisely, shook his head. He glanced upward and added, "but it's above my pay grade."

"Yeah… yeah... mine too. Dylan told me several weeks ago that he wanted to break up… wants to see other girls."

Rex inwardly fumed at that statement. He figured it was coming, but hoped it would not. Amelia and Dylan had been an item for almost two years now, and she had focused her affections exclusively on him. Rex remembered Amelia telling him many times how she had turned down an offer from this guy, another offer from that guy, many offers from many other guys. Rex could not remember all the names. She had so many opportunities to find true love or at least better love. Squandered on Dylan. She told Rex months ago that she hoped Dylan would ask her to marry him.

"What are you going to do now?"

Amelia shrugged. "I could tell that Daddy was never excited about Dylan. At least someone will be happy."

Daddy often vented to Rex, as well as Momma, his misgivings about Dylan. Wisely, he did so when Amelia was away at college. Several times he spoke of the boy's obvious insincerity, that the kid was self-centered. He nicknamed Dylan 'Gigolo Guy.' Daddy's explanation for saying nothing to Amelia was that it would only make her more intent on Dylan. Whenever he went on these rampages, Rex, unlike Amelia's mother, remained silent and let Daddy vent. Amelia's mother often argued, but the end result showed the wisdom of Rex' approach. Arguing solved nothing and left both parents frustrated. After he vented to Rex by himself, nothing was resolved, but at least Daddy felt better. Rex instinctively knew how to handle Daddy.

"What makes you say that? Your father would never be happy about anything that would make you unhappy."

Rex's observation prompted feelings of guilt to surface in Amelia. More tears ran down her cheeks.

"I know…" she replied between sobs. "You're right as always… but he will be glad that Dylan's no longer in my life."

"Maybe he thinks the hurt of breaking up is less than the hurt that comes in a bad relationship."

"Yeah. Maybe."

Amelia's tears ceased as she silently contemplated Rex's last words. Finally, he prompted her. "There's something more. Something you're not telling me."

"Yeah, there is…"

I knew the cause of Amelia's reluctance to continue. It involved a delicate subject that many young females might find embarrassing to discuss with an older male friend such as Rex. She had discussed delicate subjects with Rex in the past, but tonight was somehow different. He wisely declined to press the issue and instead waited for her to proceed when she felt more comfortable.

"Dylan wanted me to… to move in with him… live together after graduation. I knew Momma and Daddy… especially Daddy… would hit the ceiling. Momma always said, 'No ring, no benefits.' Dylan thought that was way too bourgeois. After I said no, that's when he broke up with me."

Amelia squirmed and glanced around as she spoke. Sex outside of marriage nowadays is still verboten in some traditional kingdoms, but it is not a big issue here. We are fairly sophisticated here in regards to things like that. For this reason, I knew her squeamishness specifically arose from talking about it in a public establishment with an older male friend like Rex. She feared his disapproval.

Instead, Rex said, "Knowing your parents as I do, I can imagine what they would have said. I love both of them, but your father can be hard to handle at times. He loves you so much and wants only the best for you. It's hard to say the right things sometimes when you love someone and want to protect them."

"He means well, but sometimes…" Amelia began crying, this time more emotionally.

"I know your Dad isn't the reason I see these tears," Rex spoke as he gently stroked her hand.

"Oh… oh Rex," Amelia spoke between sobs. "You always know what I'm thinking."

Rex did and nodded for her to continue.

"I thought Dylan loved me. I assumed he would want to marry me, but now… but now I realize he was just using me… for one thing. He really doesn't love me. What is there left in life worthwhile if you cannot find love?" Amelia's eyes pleaded with Rex for an answer as her sobs intensified. Rex knew she had contemplated suicide several times over the last month.

Amelia's tearful comments might surprise some as popular media portray physical sex as no big deal in the younger generation's female psyche. I knew this perception to be far from reality, especially in Amelia's case. Rex interrupted my reverie.

"Perhaps it is better to find out now that he really doesn't love you, than later when it might be more difficult to let go."

I was filled with pride at Rex's insightfulness, especially coming from someone in his seventies. His mental faculties appeared even more acute now than when he was alive. He wisely avoided responding directly to her question and instead, chose to guide her in a positive direction.

I returned my attention to their conversation.

"Yeah. I hadn't thought of that. But, it's so painful when you do find out. He'd been cheating on me even before we broke up."

"Oh?"

"Yeah. I was the only one that didn't know. My roommate told me after I came back to the room that night, crying my eyes out."

That memory brought more sobs and tears on Amelia's part. Rex was visibly moved. He said, "It pains me so much to see you suffer. Why do you think he was that way?"

"I… I don't know." Amelia's eyes widened. A confused look appeared on her face. I could tell she struggled for an answer. Next to dying, unrequited love is one of the most devastating of human experiences.

"If you were in his shoes, would you do what he did?"

"No, of course not. I'd never do that to another human being. I'd never tell someone I loved them like he did me, if I didn't really love them… lead them on just to get one thing."

Rex lowered his head perceptibly, almost ashamedly, before he spoke. I knew he remembered conquests from his younger days. He was quite popular with the females back then. He said, "Young males tend to do that sort of thing in their youth. What do you think of someone that would do that… to someone else?"

"Not much," Amelia promptly replied, having no need for thoughtful contemplation. "Anyone that would… would use someone for only sex… would trifle with someone else's love… doesn't deserve the time of day…"

Amelia abruptly stopped. Her tears had ceased. A look of discovery swept over her face much as the sun lights up the land below when a dark cloud passes on by. I knew that the confusion and ignorance in which she had lived for weeks had vanished. It pleased me that clarity and knowledge had taken over her mind. That was my hope and objective when she first opened the door to the bar.

"Oh Rex! Why didn't I think of this myself? I didn't lose someone that mattered anyway, did I?"

"Not really—"

Rex's answer was suddenly overtaken by a violent quaking. The whole world seemed to crumble, then explode. Bright light erupted. Amelia felt her body shaking vigorously.

Not Just a Dream

"Amelia. Amelia! Wake up! Wake up!"

Her brain struggled, but I knew that would only be temporary. Rex was gone, replaced by fog—only briefly and only inside her brain. Her roommate's face gradually came into view.

"Wake up! You've been talking in your sleep again."

"Uh… uhmmmm… uh… wha… wha…"

"BFF, you been dreaming. You been tossing and turning in your sleep… big time. Chattering away like a talk show host. I thought you'd never stop. And when you weren't talking, you were crying. How's a person supposed to sleep with all that going on in the room? I needed to get back to sleep. That's why I decided to wake you up."

"Yeah… yeah." Amelia slowly sat upright. She looked around and recognized her dorm room. She stretched then rotated her head in efforts to facilitate the wake-up process. "It was almost the same dream like those I've been having lately. Ya know… where I'm lost, wandering in a fog some place I've never been… can't find my way out."

"Again? Why am I not surprised? You been having that one every night it seems like for the past month. Ever since Dylan dumped you."

Her roommate eased his name out, fearing it might upset Amelia as it had done so previously. She was surprised that Amelia reacted differently tonight. No tears came. Instead of burying her face in her hands and mumbling delusions about Dylan between sobs, she looked directly into her roommate's eyes and spoke decisively, distinctly. She said, "This one tonight was different."

"Oh?!"

Amelia nodded affirmatively, and a slight smile turned up the corners of her mouth. Her eyes twinkled as she continued.

"I'm fine. No more 'Miss Morbid'. That dream made me realize Dylan is not worth the heartache."

Her roommate nodded vigorously as Amelia continued.

"I've been asking myself for weeks now. Why? Why doesn't Dylan love me as much as I love him? Why does he treat me this way? Why does this have to happen to me? Why does he want to see other girls? Why can't he just love me like I want him to?"

"I ask myself 'Why?' a lot myself… as in why couldn't I at least have gotten a C in my Algebra class?" her roommate joked.

Amelia laughed, then turned serious.

"You know my problem has been worse than that. You know that I've been asking myself why does God, if there is a God, let things like this happen? Why does he let people go through this misery?"

I knew that Amelia had discussed this topic several times in recent weeks with her roommate. Their conversations became deep and heavy into philosophy and religion. Her roommate majored in philosophy. She asked, "So, you get an answer in your dream last night?"

"No, not really. But at least I found out that the answer doesn't really matter… at least in my relationship with Dylan."

"Sounds like it was a good dream."

"It was… a great dream. Weird to the max. It started out the same as the others. I'm by myself wandering on some street some place, and it's really foggy. But then, tonight I came up on a very nice bar. I go inside, and it's very sophisticated, very cozy and comfy. And Rex is sitting there."

"Ohhhh…" Her roommate's groan resounded with heartfelt sympathy. She met Rex during Spring Break last year, and their mutual attraction was instantaneous. He died shortly after Amelia left home to go to Dylan's during her Christmas vacation. "I know it's tough. As much as I miss him, it's gotta be so much worse for you."

Suppressing tears, Amelia avoided looking directly at her roommate. She said, "Yeah. It's been three months, but I still think about him every day."

Desire to lighten Amelia's grief motivated her roommate's next comment. "Rex in a bar? That must've been a hoot."

"It was hilarious… talk about weird." Amelia shook her head and said, "Even more strange. He's sitting at a table, wearing one of those old-fashioned smoking jackets like you see in the old movies on TCM. Just like that Thin Man guy."

"Rex in a smoking jacket! That is wild, BFF. No more Ghost Pepper Tortilla Chips for you before bed."

The smoking jacket in Amelia's dream was not the most outlandish thing that Rex ever wore around her. I remembered when Amelia was much younger, during the first years after meeting Rex, he would willingly play dress up with her. Amelia suddenly recalled those same memories.

"It reminds me of when I used to dress him up when we played together. Sometimes I'd put a little bow tie around his neck and pretend we were going someplace fancy. Sometimes I'd put one of my doll's bonnets on his head and scrunch him into my stroller and take him for a walk. He looked so funny, but he never balked. Never complained. Just played along. Endured everything just like it was another one of his duties."

Eye's rolling and head nodding, her roommate turned and looked at a familiar picture of Amelia and Rex on her chest of drawers. One of Amelia's favorites, it showed her and Rex sitting in her front porch swing. A nine-year old Amelia wore a clown costume, and Rex looked very silly with a small clown hat on his head and a multi-colored bandana around his neck. The bottom of the picture was labeled 'Halloween 2007.' Amelia's eyes followed those of her roommate to the picture as well.

"We used to spend hours sitting in that swing. He loved it. I'd scratch his neck and chatter away, telling him about school, my boyfriends, my troubles, you name it, and most times he'd just sit there with his eyes closed, taking it all in. I could tell him things I would never tell anyone else. Sometimes, I'd tell him a secret, then pretend he'd talk back to me about it. He always seemed to understand. The perfect companion. You couldn't ask for a better pet."

"Next, you'll be telling me he talked to you in your dream last night."

"Yeah, he did! That's the craziest thing! I talked to him, and he talked back to me, but it seemed so realistic. Not like when I used to pretend like he was talking to me when I was little."

"A talking sheltie…" Skepticism permeated her roommate's comment. "I knew they were pretty bright, but that's what I call one smart dog."

"He was. Ya know, shelties are one of the smartest breeds of dogs there is. He seemed to understand everything I'd tell him."

"Yeah. I loved it when I'd come stay with you, and play with Rex. It seemed almost like playing with a person, he was so smart."

"When I was little, I played with him just like he was my brother or something. I dressed him up all the time. Put little baby socks on his paws, little baby bonnets on his head, handkerchiefs around his neck… God I miss him so…"

"I loved all those Halloween pictures you showed me… that dog had some pretty wild costumes."

"He was always so excited on Halloween. You could tell he enjoyed it when I dressed him in his costume. When we'd go trick-or-treating, the neighbors loved his costume. They always gave me extra treats just for him."

"You didn't feed him candy, did you?"

"No, the neighbors knew he'd be trick-or-treating with me and have special doggie treats just for him. And Rex knew he was in the spotlight those nights. He'd put on a good show for them… bark on command for a treat, sometimes do his little herding circle on the front lawn to show his appreciation for the treat. It was hilarious."

"He really had that herding instinct in him."

"For sure. Most shelties do, but his instinct was ginormous."

"He seemed so proud when he'd do them. I loved it when he'd do his herding circles for me."

"Yeah, everybody does… I mean did."

"Sounds like you had a great dream."

"It was so real. One of those dreams where when you wake up you don't know whether you were dreaming or awake. Rex was so cool. Wearing that smoking jacket, sitting in a sophisticated bar, drinking scotch, giving me sage advice. Suited Rex to a tee."

"How old was he when he died?"

"Pretty old for a sheltie. Thirteen years old. That's over seventy in dog years."

"What did you two talk about in your dream?"

"Mostly about Dylan. Rex was so helpful. It reminded me of when I was a teenager and dating. I'd sit on the front porch swing or lay in bed at night with him and talk about boys. I gabbed with him just like he was one of my girlfriends… Justin… Justin was my first real boyfriend. I was fourteen. Oh God! Was I head over heels in love with him?! Rex got an earful every night for two weeks about how great Justin was, how we were gonna get married, how much I wanted to lose my virginity to Justin."

"*Did* Justin help you lose your virginity?"

"No. That honor was reserved for Jordan, but we can talk about that later… after I've had a couple of cosmos."

"So why did you give Rex an earful about Justin for only two weeks? Sounds like a short relationship. What happened?"

"Justin and I had a fight."

"Over what?"

"Daniel Radcliffe. I thought he was soooo cute, and Justin thought he was gay. Now that I think about it, I think Rex never thought much of Justin. He got a real serious look on his face whenever I talked about him."

"Sounds like Rex gave you some good advice about Dylan last night."

"He helped me realize that Dylan isn't worth all the heartache. He's a… a typical male. Out for just one thing."

"So, is that what you meant when you said that the reason why things, like a busted relationship with Dylan, doesn't really matter?"

"Exactly. We'll probably never know why these things happen. Even Rex couldn't answer that. But they do. Like they say, 'shit happens', although Rex didn't say it in those terms. He was the consummate gentleman last night."

"He always was."

"I wish you could have been there… in my dream. You would have loved it. It was like going to some exclusive James Bond nightclub and meeting the Most Interesting Man in the World."

"Did Rex drink Dos Equis beer and say 'stay thirsty my friend' in your dream?"

"No. He was much more suave than that. You should've seen that smoking jacket. And understanding. He knew how upset I was over Dylan. He never pressed me. Only offered advice when I asked or at the right time. Just like when I used to talk to him when he was alive, but he didn't say anything back. The main thing is that I finally realized that when I lost Dylan, I didn't lose someone that mattered anyway, and that's a good thing."

"Sometimes it takes a while to work things out in your head. I should know. Anyway, it is a good thing. You've been pining and moaning over him ever since he dumped you. Like you were going off the grid when it comes to living. It's been… how long has it been?"

"Thirty-four days."

"Welcome back to the real world. Time to move on, Girl."

Heaven

"You did well. I'm pleased." I looked down at Rex and began scratching his fur in his favorite spot, right behind his ears. Rex's mouth opened, and a wide smile appeared as he panted. He still enjoyed a good scratch. If I had favorites, he would be one of them.

I never regretted granting man free will. It was either that or have a bunch of automatons. Or nothing. What fun is that, especially the second option? Every day, the same thing, over and over forever. Sure, everyone would be happy all the time, you'd know exactly what was going to happen next, but why even have human beings in that kind of a world? The downside is that it does cause suffering, a lot of it, including my own, to the extent that they make bad choices. Amelia's desire for Dylan is a case in point. Using pets like Rex is one way I found of alleviating some of that suffering.

"Your best friend looks a lot better this morning. You have indeed been good medicine for her."

Rex's head nodded in agreement. I kept scratching and praised him.

"Good boy… good boy. It truly helps someone experiencing emotional problems when I send a deceased loved one, such as yourself, to comfort them in a dream."

I remembered discussing this idea with my Kingdom's Holy Communion of Saints about seven hundred years ago. It was Saint Francis' idea to send pet animals. He enthused about how dogs would be especially helpful. Man's best friend and all that. As always, Francis was right. I remembered him addressing me with beautiful reasoning.

"O Lord, in a dream, a person troubled with woes could receive personal comfort directly from someone who never judged them in life. Someone who uncritically accepted them as they were and not as others thought they should be. A dream would reunite that person with their pet much as when the pet was alive. And, if Thou giveth the animal ability to speak in the dream, I believe that would facilitate the troubled person's healing even more. Dogs have an innate wisdom seldom appreciated whilst they live. Giving them the ability to communicate will facilitate sharing that wisdom with their troubled loved ones."

I looked down at Rex again and realized I had stopped scratching his neck. He still smiled, but knowing he wanted more, I obliged.

"Good boy."

Why Me?

What the mind doesn't understand, it worships or fears.

- *Alice Walker*

He is terribly afraid of dying because he hasn't yet lived.

- *Franz Kafka*

An Orderly World

We strolled in a perfect and orderly world. White birch provided latticed sunlight in which reds and yellows of poppy and dandelion intermingled with whites and purples of lily of the valley, lilac, and peony. Deer contentedly grazed nearby on turquoise green grass as a pair of rabbits observed. A glistening white dove winged its way overhead in the cloudless blue sky that spread across My heavens crowned with a pineapple yellow sun. The two of us strolled in a perfect world up here, but the world down there was not perfect. And a world that is not perfect is bound to be marked with disorder.

Saint Francis said, "O Lord, I worry about Craig. As Thou knowest, he is about to receive very bad news."

"It is impossible to foretell exactly how anyone will deal with bad news, especially that which Craig will be told. I would not be surprised if he does not react well. That is a risk of man's free will."

Saint Francis nodded. "I have anticipated that eventuality and have something in mind in case it should be needed."

I knew what he had in mind.

Denial and Anger

Craig had not lived yet. Not nearly long enough anyway. He was only nineteen when his parents walked into the exam room. Chrome medical instruments hanging on white sterile walls said nothing hopeful. Their son's face communicated his consternation. Wrinkles accenting his parents' forced smiles belied efforts to mask their worry. The doctor began his explanation tactfully, but it soon hardened into one cruel sentence.

"As I told him before you came in, I believe your son has a malignant brain tumor."

This ominous diagnosis came not unexpectedly. Craig's hellish odyssey began the first week home after completing his freshman year at college. A grand mal seizure as he performed kitchen duties for his mother marked its beginning. Subsequent weeks blurred within his confused brain. An appointment with a neurosurgeon, another with an oncologist, more bloodwork, more radiologic diagnostic procedures, more prodding, more questions, more of this, more of that, and "chances of survival with this type of cancer are fifty-fifty".

I knew of his emotional turmoil and his questions. *How could I have cancer? I'm too young to have cancer. Nineteen-year olds don't get cancer. I'm healthy as a horse. Other than the cancer. Why me?*

Craig never imagined anything like this ever happening to him. No one had ever prepared him for the possibility of dying. The reality of dying would soon hit him like a two-ton weight.

Treatments began shortly after his diagnosis was confirmed. A week of misery, followed by two weeks of recovery, if you could call it that. This would be the routine for most of his summer vacation. Pretty boring if it were not so terrible. Side effects—nausea, vomiting, diarrhea, fatigue, insomnia—left him wondering if the cure was worse than the cancer. Youth advantaged his body's capacity to endure the devastation but provided no such edge for ravages cancer reeks on its victims' minds. By the time the first round of treatments were over, less than half his summer vacation remained. Craig doubted he would return to experience his sophomore year.

Craig's personality changed. I knew his denial had turned into anger shortly after treatments began. *It's not fair! It's not right! I'm too young. Why me? Why would a merciful God punish me in this way?* His gregariousness gave way to sullenness and silence.

The young man's moodiness prompted his parents to suggest he look into his old high school summer job. They reasoned activity might be better than unoccupied days of introspection and believed he could handle some sort of light work in between treatment days. Accordingly, they spoke to his old boss. He was enthusiastic at having his favorite summer employee return. He laughed over the phone, recalling Craig's demolition of a Nabisco display the first time he operated the grocery store's massive floor scrubber.

"Of course, he can come back to work," he said. "Craig was the best stock boy I ever had.

Such a good, hard worker. Not many have his work ethic nowadays. A fine young man. What a sense of humor! He kept all of us entertained. I don't think I'll ever forget his dance rendition of that Beyoncé song *Single Ladies* one night after all the customers were gone. Craig did a dance karaoke to it in the Produce Section. I wish someone would have thought to video it, but we were all too busy laughing."

Craig went to work, performed as best he could, but his moods were not lost on fellow employees. They saw that the Craig that was needed for a spill on aisle twelve this summer was not the same Craig that danced to *Single Ladies* last summer. This person possessed little of the zest and spirit of the old Craig. This was an angry, withdrawn person. Among themselves, they discussed his periodic volcanic-like outbursts. Their outward signs of sympathy had no effect. They were worried.

Saint Francis and I also worried. He said, "I'll do something tonight."

House of Fortune

Craig furiously stomped down the same pathway he had trod on for nights. The path leading to a closed door. Each night, he twisted and pulled on the door knob to no avail. His anger swelled the more his attempts failed. His oncologist explained these kinds of dreams often happened to people with cancer. They were a side effect of a sleep aid prescribed to address the insomnia often accompanying cancer treatments.

He wanted to enter but feared what lay inside. *Something is going on in there that affects me. What if it's the answer to my question? Why me?*

Tonight, the door knob yielded to Craig's efforts. A small room greeted him with walls that could best be described as splotchy cerulean blue. An Impressionistic painting of three sailboats on troubled waters under dark, cloudy skies served as a focal point for the wall directly opposite the door. To the paintings' right, an old grandfather clock displayed the time as two o'clock.

Seven chairs surrounding a large round table, all of simple design, comprised the room's only other furniture. Green felt bonded to its top surface indicated this was a card table as did several piles of poker chips. Six of its seven chairs were occupied by non-human players, all with glasses of beer in front of them.

Craig instantly recognized the setting. The print in his father's study! He racked his brain. *Dogs something. Dogs in need. A friend in need. Dogs playing poker. That's it! Dogs Playing Poker!* That was what this room was all about. It was the scene from the print his father always called *Dogs Playing Poker*. That name actually applied to an old series of paintings about dogs engaging in a variety of human games and activities, while the one in his father's study was titled *A Friend in Need.*

He scanned the card players left to right. Furthest left, a tri-color Border Collie held his cards close and must have had a good hand as a sly smile adorned his face. To his left, or his right as viewed by Craig, a black Poodle sat, her cards also held high. *Funny, the picture in Dad's study has a Saint Bernard next to the Collie instead of a Poodle.* The Poodle's worried expression reveals something about her card luck. Ah, those emotional French!

In seats immediately in front of and closest to Craig sat two dogs. Leftmost and same as in his dad's print is a solid red Bulldog wearing a spiked collar. To his right is a Rottweiler. The Bulldog sits with his back to Craig while the Rottweiler sits sort of sideways. This is so he can surreptitiously pass an ace with his paw underneath the table to the Bulldog, whose paw already contains three aces. *Same scenario as in Dad's print.*

Centered between these two, but sitting across the table from them, a classic black and tan German Shepherd faces Craig. *Isn't that place taken by another Saint Bernard in the print?*

Something else differs. To the Shepherd's left, chair number six, is vacant. Next to it and as viewed by Craig the seat furthest right is not occupied by the same dog as in his dad's painting. Instead, a Golden Retriever wearing an aqua and orange bandana emblazoned with a Miami Dolphins logo sits there.

"Tucker!" Craig shouted.

His old pal died six years ago at the ripe old age of twelve, only a year younger than Craig was at the time. In some ways, Tucker appeared the same as last remembered. His fur coat mimicked a field of wheat, not only in its amber color but also in the way it flowed over his skin in wisps and waves, as if blown by a gusty wind. An ear-to-ear smile still dominated a large, friendly face. The smile was unmistakably Tucker through and through.

Craig also noticed some physical differences. The dog's brown, almond eyes lacked quite the sparkle the young man remembered. His face had sprinkles of grey throughout as did the top of his head and neck. His natural aging lent a touch of wisdom to a face that bespoke strength and courage.

Tucker belonged to one of Craig's neighbors, and each morning for as long as Craig could remember, the Retriever's mom tied a red paisley cowboy bandana around his neck. The result—an absolutely adorable effect on such a massive dog.

Craig could not resist commenting on the new look. "I see you're wearing a little different outfit today. What's up?"

"I was at a Dolphins game today. The fans beside me couldn't resist," Tucker said. He performed his own appraisal of his old friend. Craig appeared taller than remembered.

Although the young man's facial characteristics had matured, Tucker still recognized the same handsome countenance. Dark brown, almost black, wavy hair crowned thick eyebrows that offset mocha eyes. Women, especially those over the age of thirty, always commented on his gorgeously long eyelashes. However, the thing most appreciated no longer existed. The young man's blemish-free, olive-toned face was now pale from chemotherapy.

Dog sitting and walking Tucker was one of Craig's first paying jobs, but unlike his summer job mowing lawns, he performed this task year-round. This occurred frequently as Tucker's mom and dad were often out of town visiting their grown children. Boy and dog grew close over the twelve years they knew each other.

The large animal, as befitting his breed, was as gentle as a lamb, with one exception that Craig vividly remembered. Twice in performance of his dog sitting duties, the young boy opened the backdoor in Tucker's house only to find a dead rabbit that the canine had dutifully deposited nearby outside. *Canis familiaris* and *canis lupus* share the same genus after all.

Despite the rabbit incidents, Tucker was not a vicious dog. His even-tempered, naturally calm and collected disposition fit the Golden Retriever mold to a tee. He manifested another of his breed's traits, sociability, through his affinity for human beings. One would have to look far and wide to find a human being the dog disliked. Tucker only wanted to be one of the guys and pal around with you, which is a reason the breed is not known for its credentials as a guard dog. Those people he really loved became part of his pack.

"Who won the game?" Craig asked.

"Don't know. Had to leave after the start of the first half to get here on time. Why don't you come over here and sit beside me?" he asked, a touch of Scottish brogue in his speech. He pointed to the vacant chair next to him, nodded to the Border Collie, and added a fateful phrase. "Time to deal him in."

Why Me?

"What is this all about?" Craig asked as he slid into his chair.

Without looking at the young man, the Border Collie began scooping up everyone's cards and said with his best Northumberland accent, "This is a game of fortune, old boy. A game of chance. Five card poker, nothing wild. You are going to play."

"What am I playing for?" Craig's question was rhetorical. His gut told him what his stakes were.

"Something very important, *mon ami*," the Poodle said. "Your most valuable possession."

Craig correctly guessed the French phrase meant 'my friend' despite not having taken that language his freshman year in college. He noticed the dog's nervous tapping the table top with her paws.

Is that impatience? Craig had played poker with his college roommates and knew impatience was not characteristic of a good card player. Maybe a symptom of the breed's high strung nature? Whatever it was, it prompted Craig to think, *she's either not a good poker player or resentful at having to be here in the first place. That makes two of us.* He asked, "But why do I have to play? Why me?"

"Mate, I wish I knew the answer to that one, but it's above my pay grade." The Bulldog ruefully shook his head. Not the most intelligent canine at the table, but he at least knew his place in the scheme of things.

The Rottweiler nodded concurrence, then held his paws up rather melodramatically. I knew his ostentatious hand waving to be a remnant of the breed's Italian origins. His overly dramatized gestures accompanied his proclamation. "The truth is that we don't *exactly* know why people come here."

"*Ya, mein* friend," the Shepherd said, "but we do know who comes here because we have seen them with our own eyes."

All business, the Collie finished shuffling and began dealing cards. He glanced at the Shepherd and said, "But old bean, we don't see who doesn't come here."

Craig picked up his first card, a six of clubs. *Whoop-de-doo. Not.*

“Or if there are some that don’t ever come here,” added the Poodle.

Despite these comments, the Shepherd would not be deterred. He vigorously shook his head. “Doesn’t matter. We know we see a lot of people come in here. All kinds. All sizes, shapes, colors, genders, gender preferences, ages, even the unborn… been seeing more of those lately… but I’m getting off track. Anyway, you name it. If you ask me, I think everyone comes here to play sooner or later.”

The Bulldog intently stared at Craig, evaluating the new player. “You’re no different from anyone else that’s come through here so far.”

“Thanks… thanks for nothing.” Craig spat out the words. *I’ve had nothing but bad luck for months, and you tell me I’m no different than anyone else. How many people do I know that have cancer?* He picked up his second card, a three of clubs. *Not necessarily a good card in and of itself, but maybe a chance for some sort of a flush?*

Tucker finally spoke. “I understand your anger, my old friend. Let me assure you that’s a waste of time. Anger gets you nothing and nowhere. I know. I used to get pissed off at vacuum cleaners all the time. Always making that awful noise and darting back and forth in front of me. Guess what? Didn’t do a bit of good. They’re still around and still being obnoxious.”

That is so Tucker, Craig thought, remembering how the dog loved teasing others by playing keep away with Squeaky, his rubber mouse. His playfulness could always make you forget your troubles. Craig bit his lip and nodded. "I know you're right. I know. I guess it's just my bad luck. What did the doctor say? My chances are fifty-fifty. Just bad luck."

"Not exactly luck, old boy," the Border Collie said as he dealt another round of cards. "Something akin to it but different. Something most people cannot fathom. That's what 'luck' is."

Craig's mind expanded on his original 'Why me?' question. *Why would a rational Greater Being allow such things to occur without some reason beyond simple chance?*

"Tell us what's on your mind, my old friend," Tucker said.

"I'm just having difficulty understanding why God does what he does," the young man said. He picked up his third card, another club. This time a seven. He bit his tongue to prevent the smile his lips wanted to set free as the Collie continued dealing.

The Poodle picked up her fourth card and placed it with the others, close to her chest. Craig noticed a hint of chagrin in her expression. *Looks like I was right about her poor poker skills.*

As she put her cards face down in front of her, she said, "A lot of us do, *mon chu*. Why do we get the cards we get? Why do things happen the way they do? A lot of people try to guess why. But it does not matter anyway. As they say, poop happens. That's the way it is. Death and the various ills sometimes caused by man's free will are unavoidable."

"Why? Why does it have to be that way?" Craig asked as his fourth card landed face down in front of him. He fought to keep his hands from trembling as he picked it up. It was a four of clubs. *One card away from a possible flush, maybe even a straight flush!* A five of clubs would give him straight flush, the highest hand possible in this game of poker!

Tucker looked at the Collie, perhaps the most intelligent player at the table, as he picked up his fourth card. He said, "My old friend has a good question. You want to take it?"

"I'd be honored," the Collie said. He paused in dealing cards and turned to Craig. "Take free will for example, old man. God allows man to have free will, so bad things sometimes happen."

"Why does it have to be that way?"

"What other way would you have it? Have it so each person only did exactly what God wanted them to do?"

Craig shrugged. "No… I guess not…"

"Rather boring situation that would be if you ask me," said the Rottweiler. "Not just for God, but also for people."

The canine looked up from his cards as he finished speaking, and Craig saw two loving eyes staring at him. *Maybe I've misjudged*

Rottweilers. I thought they were vicious dogs. He said, “Yeah. I guess it would.”

Tucker said, “Life really wouldn’t be worth living if things were that way.”

The Collie resumed dealing cards, tossing the Poodle her fifth and last card. He looked at Craig and said, “My good chap, free will allows man to make his own decisions, do what he wants to. Sometimes that works out pretty well, but sometimes it does not.”

From Craig’s silent shrug, I knew he needed more convincing. To My delight, his old friend stepped up to the plate.

“Remember when you were about four or five, and they gave you that toy robot for Christmas?” Tucker asked.

“Yeah,” the young man replied. As best he could remember, it was about a foot high and had three buttons that made it talk or move, or do both at the same time, depending on which combination of buttons you pushed. “I remember you thoroughly enjoyed it whenever I brought it over to your house.”

“You gave it to my mom and dad about a week after you got it for Christmas.”

“Yeah. You enjoyed it so much, I wanted you to have it to play with all the time.”

“But *why* did you give it to them and not just keep bringing it over with you?”

Craig paused, thinking back. He was five when it happened, but the memories slowly returned. He said, “I think I got bored with it.

After I figured out what buttons made it do certain things, it got old."

"It got predictable, didn't it?" asked the Shepherd right after he picked up his fifth card.

Craig turned his head to get a better view of the Shepherd's facial expression but got no clue from it as to the makeup of his hand. He said, "Yes. It did."

"You got bored with it because it became predictable. Same way with God. Free will keeps man from being predictable."

"Okay, I concede on all of everyone's points about free will, but why do people have to die? Why do I have to die?"

"It works this way my good chap," the Collie said, dealing the young man his last card. Craig took no note of the card as the canine continued. "Death is a part of life, part of the ongoing process of decay. Everything decays, both living and nonliving things. Decay is a physical process required by the laws of physics that control operation of the universe."

The Poodle could tell that from the Bulldog's facial expression that he was having trouble following the Collie's explanation. With a face like his, who could tell? She looked at him and explained, "Physics—molecules and atoms and things like that doing what they do."

I knew that it was much more complicated than that, but I applauded her efforts to make it more understandable to the humble canine.

"What does this have to do with why I have to die at this point in time?" Craig asked, shaking his head.

"God created the universe using the laws of physics," the Shepherd said. I detected a touch of pride in his voice and knew he was honored to be following in the footsteps of the great German physicist, Albert Einstein. "Physics requires decay, and death is part of the process of decay."

"That was good, but it didn't address his question," the Poodle said. "He wants to know why he has to play a game of chance right now."

The Collie, having dealt every player their fifth and last card, took a deep breath. "Look at it this way, old bean. The process of decay, which is governed by the physics of matter, says that people have to eventually die. Got that?"

Craig nodded.

"Now, put yourself in God's place. You don't want some sort of predictable by the book process for determining when people die. That gets back to the discussion we just finished on man's free will and predictability and boring processes. So, if you're God, what do you do? What else but throw chance into the mix?"

"And your point is?" Craig asked. He still had not picked up his fifth card.

The Bulldog's simple mind stepped up to the plate. He said, "Creating the Universe required laws of physics to do so. Math is a part of physics. Math has many components like algebra, geometry, and for our purposes, the field of statistics and probability. Luck or chance or whatever you want to call it is nothing but an application of probability. It's simple, mate. He uses one of His existing tools to introduce unpredictability into the process of determining when people die."

Excellent! Spot on! Good work, My friend!

"You're saying that chance or luck alone determines when we die?" asked Craig.

"No, of course not," replied the Rottweiler. He had been quiet for a while, so I was glad to see him get back into the conversation. "People can influence the decay process by the choices they make just like they can influence any process in which randomness plays a role. But they can't completely circumvent it."

Luck of the Draw

"Lady and Gentlemen, it's getting late," said the Collie, nodding at the grandfather clock, which indicated the time was almost five thirty. "We need to play poker. You can draw up to three replacement cards. Lowest hand loses."

Craig looked at his hand. It contained a three, four, six, and seven of clubs. *Any club besides a five gives me a flush. What are the odds of that? With all those hearts, spades, and diamonds out there—not good. A five of clubs gives me a straight flush. What are the odds of that? One in a million?* The young man's negative thoughts were palpable, so much so that the other players sensed his gloom. Dogs are incredibly perceptive with regards to a human being's emotions. In fact, I knew the odds of getting a flush in poker to be one in 509 and a straight flush to be one in 72,193. Craig's hand shook as he picked up his last card.

A Queen of Hearts… worthless for his hand. He had nothing. No pairs, no flush, no straight, no nothing. The lowest hand possible. He looked up from his cards, not attempting to keep his poker face.

"How many?" the Collie asked the Poodle.

"*Trois*," she said, giving Craig hope that her hand was not that good.

The Collie dealt her three cards, then looked at the Shepherd who said, "three."

After the Shepherd received his cards, Craig hesitated. *Should I draw one card in hopes it will be a four of clubs, or at least a club? The only alternative to that is to draw three cards and maybe get something that will result in a pair, maybe two pairs.* He held up his forefinger, and the Collie tossed a single card to him face down. He was too fearful to look at it even after he picked it up.

"One card, if you please, my good man," Tucker said.

Craig shot a sideways glare at his old friend. *That doesn't sound good for me. He seems awfully cavalier. How nice for you.*

The Rottweiler completed the process by saying, "One card."

Craig willed himself to look down at his new card. *A ten of diamonds!* His heart fell again. He still had nothing, the lowest combination of cards and worth nothing. His mind raced. *Maybe someone else will have a hand this bad. Otherwise...*

The Collie looked at the Poodle. He said, "Show us what you got."

She laid down her cards one by one. A Jack of diamonds, a Jack of spades… Craig did not bother to look at the rest of her cards. Instead, he focused on the Shepherd who laid down a three of hearts, a three of diamonds… Craig's heart sank again. Both canines had better hands than his. His turn to reveal his hand was at hand. He thought about throwing his cards down and running away but was afraid of the consequences. He felt a nudge on his thigh and glanced down. Tucker's paw pressed against him, underneath the table so no one else could see. A card was sandwiched between the dog's big toes.

Dumb Luck

Craig's father smiled. A forced smile bred from months-long habit. Parents of a child with a deadly illness learn to do that. It does no one any good, especially the sick child, if everyone is gloomy all the time. He said, "It's almost six o'clock. Slept late this morning, didn't you? A good thing. You probably needed it. You talked a lot in your sleep. Sounded like a TV talk show host. Must have been some dream."

"Yeah," Craig nodded as he sat down. "A doozy."

"Mom's almost got breakfast ready. Pour you some juice?" Knowing the son, his father began pouring before receiving an answer. "What was it about?"

"You know that picture in your study—*Dogs Playing Poker*? I was playing poker with them, although it wasn't exactly the same group of dogs. Tucker was there."

"Tucker? You mean the Lowe's old dog?"

"Yeah. That Tucker. Anyway, I'm about to lose, but Tucker slips me a five of clubs, and I lay down a straight flush to win the hand."

A Predictable World

We saw Tucker lumbering toward us from a distance. His golden coat shone beautifully in the sunshine, amber waves of fur constantly rolling across his back as he drew nigh. Sunlight seemed to sparkle as it bounced off his fur. Dogs have a way of brightening any environment they enter.

I looked down at him as he stopped and sat at my feet. I said, "Good job. You did exactly what I wanted."

I resumed walking. Saint Francis fell in on one side and Tucker on the other.

“Chance. Luck. Probability,” I said. “Call it what you will, but sometimes it works well, sometimes not so well.”

“My Lord?” asked Saint Francis.

“Sometimes, the best way is to influence things a bit.”

“Dost Thou mean cheat?”

“Call it cheating if you want. I call it influencing things. Whatever. I don’t want Craig right now.”

Saint Francis nodded. “So be it. Just as man can influence the process of decay with his choices, so can My Lord influence death.”

I looked down at Tucker. “Let’s go down and watch the second half of the Dolphins game.”

Why Not Me?

Anyone who's a parent dreads that call in the middle of the night. I have four grown children and I still dread it.

- Tony Dungy

The reason dying is so easy is because death has no meaning...

- Janne Teller

Midnight Hour

The clock displayed seventeen minutes past midnight. Billy stared at the screen, but words still refused to come. The right words never came, apparently. Four years and nothing but form letter rejections, all of which contained the same verbiage, like the one he received in his email that afternoon.

"Thank you for giving me a chance to consider your work. Unfortunately, I don't believe I'm the right agent to represent your submission effectively. Publishing is subjective by nature so don't be discouraged. Another agent may well feel differently. I wish you the best of luck finding an agent who can represent your work with the enthusiasm it deserves."

Yeah, right. Thanks for nothing. No wonder he dreaded opening emails from literary agents. Why couldn't they at least provide a modicum of feedback like one he received last month.

"I'm sorry, but your project does not sound like a fit for me at this time, and so I will have to pass. I love the premise, but not the first page. Sorry, thank you for considering me, and best of luck with your future queries."

I knew he viewed each rejection as more evidence of non-existence of a Divine Being.

Billy leaned back in his chair. His exhaustion went beyond a physical state of being. Mental weariness eviscerated his brain. Writing as an avocation was obviously going nowhere. His eyes looked skyward at the bland white popcorn ceiling. No inspiration there. He shook his head in another unconscious display of negativism.

Three novels, each rejected by a host of literary agents, takes a toll on one's psyche. The question, *Why do I continue to subject myself to this abuse?* again cycled through his brain. He knew the answer. *Neither monetary reward, fame, nor self-gratification motivates this self-abuse.* He mostly avoided thinking about the real motivation, having found doing so to be a sad and self-destructive effort.

It must have been like this for Craig. His son wanted to be a writer for as long as Billy could remember. He remembered reading his son's work and providing feedback, which became less and less negative as his son's writing improved. Billy thought his last effort, *The Sequestered Nook*, was an imaginative and beautiful short story with a twist at the end that was priceless. Yet for all his efforts, Craig received nothing but rejections similar to those now populating Billy's inbox.

Admiration swept through his brain at the thought of his son's determination. The young man knew writing was a tough, competitive business but kept on trying nonetheless. *The Sequestered Nook should have been published dammit!*

Weariness slogging through Billy's brain would soon bring some respite from frustration. His eyelids drooped, his head slumped, and sleep overtook his consciousness.

The Slug

Something was wrong. No, wrong seemed too harsh a word, and nowadays, Billy agonized over the right words. Not normal sounded better. The objects greeting him as he walked through his kitchen into his garage—Bassett breakfast table, Whirlpool stove, Maytag washer and dryer, Toyota sedan—existed back in Virginia where he lived until ten years ago, not where he lived today. These things sequenced a beginning of something that no longer happened, thank God.

His morning commute comprised half of a three-hour weekday drudgery that occurred over a five-year period. Five dreary years in which his morning misery was only exceeded by that of the evening drive back. During this period, Billy defined 'dismal' as thirty minutes driving bumper-to-bumper at 75 miles per hour followed by at least forty-five minutes of stop-and-go traffic, punctuated at least once a week by a multiple vehicle pileup that completely stopped all movement for a minimum of forty-five minutes. Worst of all, it was mostly the same thing over and over. Boring.

As he approached his car, Billy recited other reasons why he dreaded commuting to downtown Washington. *Wasted time, awful local radio stations, rude Beltway drivers, let me count the ways.* He remembered his life back then as a monotonous, never-ending drab existence that began at oh-dark-thirty and ended about nine o'clock at night when his wife woke him up and told him to go to bed. *Does one have a life while commuting?* Good question. Billy thought of that old Peggy Lee song, *Is That All There Is?* Is that all there is to life while commuting?

Opening the Toyota's door, he also remembered one of his standard jokes at that time was that the only thing he dreaded more than a visit to the dentist was his daily commute to work.

If this is a dream, then it must be a nightmare, he speculated. *Hopefully, it will end soon.*

This commute started as they always did back then. He backed out of his garage, drove out of his development, and followed Old Plank Road to Route 3 where he stopped at the Wawa for gas and coffee. After his Wawa stop, something different occurred.

He pulled into one of the commuter parking lots scattered throughout northern Virginia. The state provided these lots to encourage carpooling, something that did not work out well for Billy due to his unpredictable work schedule. This morning, however, he felt motivated to pick up a 'slug'. These were commuters who waited in commuter lots, available to occupy a seat in cars of drivers wanting to drive in the High Occupancy Vehicle lanes on the interstate. He eased into the line of cars in the 'slug lane,' and within a minute, it was his turn to pick up one of those waiting in line for a ride.

His passenger door opened, and an old friend jumped inside.

"Sophie?!"

"Dad!" Sophie never called him 'Dad' when she was alive. She never called him anything as dogs don't talk while they live. "I'm going to ride with you this morning."

Sophie was Craig's dog, until he died four years ago. After that, she divided her loyalties between Billy and his wife, until the black and tan dachshund herself died six months ago. She passed peacefully at the ripe old age of seventeen after a gradual, nine-month decline in health. To say Sophie had a loving personality would be an understatement. She adored every human that entered her presence, even strangers once they had passed her smell test, and was equally loved in return. The volume of sympathy cards received after she passed testified to widespread affection for the little 'doxie.'

Billy stared transfixed at the last being in the world he expected to be his 'slug'. Memories arose of misery whenever they had to take her anywhere in the car. She never balked at getting in but would whine incessantly after the ignition was turned on. Her whining continued until the car's motor was turned off. It was as if she was afraid of some evil being inside the running motor.

"But Sophie, you always hated riding in cars. Remember how you'd bark and whine? It was like you were being tortured. Why are you here now?"

"Because you need my help. Now, close this door for me, and let's get the show on the road, or you'll be late for whatever it is you used to do with yourself when you left me every day."

Out of habit, Billy obeyed. Sophie invariably got her way in her relationships, both human and canine. She was, as with most dachshunds, a stubborn little dog. She was the acknowledged alpha in Billy's family. This not to say that she was not loyal, which she was. Whenever Billy assumed the sick role, Sophie eagerly joined him on the couch for a day of old movies—truly a devoted dachshund. Nevertheless, she ruled the roost at home. Her alpha personality dominated other canines as well. It always amused Billy to watch the neighbors' much larger golden retriever kowtow to her commands.

He drove in silence for several minutes, trying to wrap his mind around the fact that she had spoken to him. Her voice was not what he would have expected, had he expected anything other than whining. It reminded him of Marlene Dietrich's voice—husky, deep in the lower registers, and a distinctly Teutonic accent noted by ill-pronunciation of the letter 'r'. In Sophie's case, ending 'r's in 'door' and 'for' were mostly dropped, while 'road' became 'uwoad', 'whatever' became 'wadeva', 'yourself' became 'yossef', and 'every' became 'evawee'.

In the front passenger seat, Sophie sat quietly, as Billy glanced in her direction. She looked back, her brown sparkling eyes urging him to communicate.

"This must be a dream. I must be dreaming," he said.

"So what? Dreams sometimes help when reality falters."

Despite her pronunciation of "dweams" and "uweality", Sophie's insightful comment impressed Billy. She always was one clever little dog, typical of the dachshund breed.

"So, you're here because I need your help. Is that why you've been visiting Mom in her dreams? Because she needs help?"

Billy's wife experienced half a dozen such dreams since Sophie's death. They were the kind where you wake up not knowing whether you had dreamed or if it really happened. His wife said Sophie grrr'd and rolled around at the foot of the bed in some, and in others she heard the little dog barking elsewhere in the house.

"Not really, Dad. I just like to check on Mom once in a while. We've always been close… just like Craig and me."

Sophie looked much the same as he remembered. Some grey fur sprinkled amongst the tan in her snout and front paws. Otherwise, the rest of her fur still shined black and tan. Billy remembered another of his standard jokes—his assertion that Sophie inherited her lack of grey from his side of the family. Craig sometimes joked that she got her black fur from the same genes that produced his dark black hair. Billy immediately regretted that thought just as a red, blue, yellow and white oval sign flashed by outside the passenger window. Sophie jumped up, pressing her front paws against the passenger window.

"Look, Dad. There's a DQ. Let's go through the drive-thru and get a Peanut Buster Parfait."

PBPs were Sophie's favorite treat, and her question brought back a flood of memories. Warm Sunday afternoons. His entire family scrunched together in their old red Ford pickup truck. Sophie sat on young Craig's lap while he ordered a PBP at the DQ drive-thru to share with her. Their Mom's invariable comment questioning the sanitariness of such action. Billy wiped away some of the wetness that had accumulated around his eyes.

"Oh sweetie, I would love to get you one, but that DQ isn't open yet. It's too early in the morning."

Not the right thing to say to an alpha dachshund. Sophie lowered her head and emitted a low grrr, followed by a solitary whimper. Billy immediately did what comes naturally to dachshund owners. He offered her an alternative.

"Look, I'll tell you what. There's a DQ close to my office. It should be open by the time we get there. I'll get you one then. Okay?"

"Thanks, Dad. I knew you'd figure something out. You always did. You are the best dad a dog could have. I used to brag about you to all my friends."

Flattery normally aroused Billy's suspicion, which was his first impulse in this case. He quickly realized she spoke in earnest as dogs are intellectually unable to be insincere. Her comment reminded him of what a valued member of the family she had been.

She always seemed to understand our moods, he thought. Happy when they were happy and sad when they were sad, she seemed empathetic when empathy was needed despite, or perhaps because of her alpha status. Curiously, she had adapted over the last four years to Craig's absence much better than anyone else in the family. Billy sometimes wondered if this was because she sat on Craig's bed as the young man grew cold.

Sensing his thoughts, Sophie interrupted.

"How have you been, Dad?"

It took a moment to figure out how to avoid really answering.

"Eh… okay as usual, I guess. Not much changed since you left us. Mom's still busy with her ladies' club. We do Facetime with Cricket… almost every day. I'm still writing… with no success. Same as always at golf… still haven't broken a hundred…" Billy forgot to mention that not breaking a hundred applied to only nine holes instead of eighteen.

Sophie nodded in sympathy. Billy's golf game stank, had always stunk, and had not improved over the last four years since his retirement. He admitted golf was a dual edged sword—a source of both frustration for him and bonding with Craig. The father and son spent many Saturday mornings on the golf course, inventing new 'Billy Golf' rules as they played. Playing 'Billy Golf' allowed Billy to improve his score so as to avoid embarrassment when asked by others what it was. That thought tickled him, resulting in a smile.

As they merged into high-speed traffic on the interstate, Sophie swayed back and forth, propelled by their car's maneuvering.

"Dad! I don't like this. Have you thought about driving lessons?"

Billy bit his tongue at her pronunciation of 'dwiving'.

"Don't blame my driving. You never liked riding in any vehicle."

Except when it was in line at a DQ drive-thru. He remembered times when they would get together with their friends who owned (probably not an accurate term) two red smooth coat dachshunds, now also deceased. They would all pile in their friends' SUV and treat the three of them to PBPs.

"Remember going to the DQ with Puddin' and Bart?" he asked. "Watching you three share a couple of PBPs was always a sight to behold."

"Puddin' was a pig when it came to PBPs. She barely left any for me and Bart."

"I don't think she was quite that bad. Anyway, you three cracked us up when you chased each other around the house. Nothing beats the sight of a pack of weenie dogs racing across a polished wood floor."

"Those were the days. The three of us had so much fun together. We still do."

Billy bit his tongue again, this time at the her pronunciation of 'thwee'. He feigned not hearing her last sentence.

Sophie circled three times in the passenger seat before settling down into her canine 'safe nesting' position. Canine psychologists speculate this is done to make the ground more accommodating when they lie down as well as to perform a 360° security check. I knew the sight of her doing that would be comforting to Billy as well as Sophie. Finished, she quizzed him again.

"How have you been, Dad? Be honest this time."

How to answer her question? How to avoid answering her question honestly? I knew the intent behind Sophie's question was to get him to open up about Craig, something Billy assiduously avoided because he knew that it would lead to memories, heartache, and tears. He had found over the last four years that he could think about Craig for thirty seconds or so and be okay. Anything much more than that, and sadness overwhelmed the good thoughts and that resulted in nothing, except tears. In his mind it was no good, nothing positive ever came of it, so he decided long ago to limit his mental sessions involving Craig. That way, he managed to limit his major crying binges to only once every two or three months.

"Dad? Dad! Earth to Dad."

"I'm good… all right… keeping busy…" In a narrow sense, this was correct. Billy forced a smile and a stale quip before his voice trailed off. "Trying to stay out of your Mom's hair."

"You and Mom seem to be enjoying Cricket."

Their four-year old granddaughter's nickname resulted from the mash-up of Craig and the suffix -ette; i.e., Craigette or 'little female Craig'. She was their only granddaughter, birthed and nicknamed by their daughter Amelia, who was their only other child besides Craig. Cricket's birth occurred almost nine months after Craig's death. Billy often thought the timing of her birth uncanny.

"She's been a Godsend…" Billy was unable to complete his thought.

"Kind of gives meaning to life, doesn't it?"

As he glanced at Sophie, Billy' jaw tightened as it did when he strained to hold back tears. He remained silent. She looked up at him the way she used to when sitting on the couch with him at night. Their nightly routine during her last four years began after Billy finished his 'Dish Fairy' chores; i.e., washing dishes. She accompanied him to the Man Cave and hung out with him while he read or they both watched TV.

Billy smiled at something this memory surfaced. He occasionally speculated to others that Sophie was smart enough to learn how to read but did not do so because she figured others would perform that task for her. Other dachshund owners would always add, “as befitting her status as a dachshund,” to his speculation. He next remembered how she loved watching old *Lassie* reruns on TV Land, but slept through most other shows. Reaching over and stroking her fur, he never noticed the sign. Sophie did, and once again jumped up and threw herself repeatedly against the passenger window in a frenzy.

“Dad! Dad! Look! Look, Dad! Look! There’s another DQ sign! See it?! See it?!”

“That’s not the one, sweetie. That’s not the one. We can’t stop at that one. We missed the exit off the interstate. Be patient. We’ll be there shortly.”

Craig

They rode in silence for a while. This part of the commute took them through mostly woods that occupied the geography between Falmouth and Potomac Mills. Until the first traffic slowdown that usually occurred after Potomac Mills, it would be smooth sailing at seventy-five miles an hour. In the total darkness of four o’clock in the morning, nothing else besides other car headlights appeared visible.

Outside the car's windows, the darkness itself seemed unlimited, never ending, monotonous. Billy felt as if they rode in a rocket, hurtling alone through the vastness of space. He remembered always feeling this way during his commuting days. Nothing else existed in the universe. During this part of the commute, he used to think he was doomed to a life of endless commuting until the day he died. *I could not imagine a more boring existence.*

"You made this trip a long time, didn't you?"

"Yeah. Five years."

"That's a long time by my reckoning, isn't it, Dad?"

"Well, that would be about thirty-five dog-years, if you use the old-fashioned measure of seven dog years equals one human year."

"Wow…"

"The few times I carpooled, I rode with people who made the DC commute for twenty, even thirty human years."

"Wow! And it takes so long to drive it."

Billy looked at the clock on his dash. They had been on I-95 almost twenty minutes.

"It does take a long time to get to and from work every day. I remember thinking at the time how it seemed to be something that would never end. I figured I'd be one of those commuters who did it until the day I died. It was a depressing thought. God, how I dreaded that commute."

After her last DQ sighting, Sophie had not completely settled back down but now did so, circling once again in her seat, again looking for a 'safe nesting' position. Once this task was completed, she looked up at Billy.

"This seat is not nearly as comfortable as my pallet."

Is there anything that a dachshund won't complain about? She referred to a dark brown corduroy pallet the family used to keep by the fireplace in their living room, just for her and her occasional canine visitor. She used it so much that she wore a comfortable permanent indentation into the rectangular cushion. Craig bought it as a present for her seventh birthday shortly after they moved from Virginia.

Billy's jaw muscles tightened again. He consciously tried to direct his thoughts elsewhere and noticed he had never turned on the radio.

"Craig's fine, Dad. He was the first one waiting for me."

Despite further jaw tightening, a tear emerged. He bit his lower lip.

"He looks great. He looks thinner than the last time you saw him."

His physicians attributed Craig's weight gain to some of the cancer medications he took.

"He tastes as good as ever."

Billy smiled at the memory of Sophie vigorously licking Craig's face. He would wrap his big hands around her body and hold her inches from his nose so she could enjoy something all dogs do for their own pleasure. Canine psychologists say that the act of licking releases pleasurable endorphins in dogs and often gives them a sense of comfort and security. Dogs also sometimes lick because their saliva has antibacterial healing powers. Billy's wife sometimes speculated that Sophie was trying to heal Craig's tumor.

"Otherwise, he pretty much looks the same."

More images of Craig drifted through Billy's brain. His dark wavy hair, cut in a short crop on top and mid-fade on sides and back. Unmistakable olive skin. Did he get that from the Cherokee on his mother's side or possibly some Mediterranean genes somewhere else in the family? Thick brown eyebrows accentuating deep brown eyes. Blemish-free skin reminiscent of a young Elvis Presley. He savored these images for a while but soon wanted more.

"So, what did Craig say to you when you saw him again?"

"He shouted my name, picked me up, and put me on his shoulders like in the movie."

One of Craig's favorite movies was *The Adventures of Robin Hood* with Errol Flynn. Craig used to drape Sophie behind his neck in mock imitation of the scene where Flynn enters the castle with a deer draped around his neck and shoulders. It was one of Craig's running physical gags and got a huge laugh every time he did it. Billy could not help but chuckle at that image.

"Craig enjoyed playing with you. I remember when we first brought you home how excited he was. You were so small. Remember how he used to stuff you into the front of his shirt? He'd walk around with just your little head sticking out between the buttons. Your paws never touched the ground the first two years of your life."

Painful thoughts interrupted the humorous image.

Oh, to be able to be with Craig right now. To see him again. Hug him one last time. To talk to him again if only for one more hour.

I felt Billy's heartache and desperately hoped he would receive at least some modicum of comfort from this drive with Sophie.

"He was my best friend while he was alive. Remember when you first brought me home to live with you. I was to be Craig's dog. You thought I'd sleep on that baby blanket in that little cardboard box beside his bed."

"Yeah. What a joke. We found you two cuddled up together on the floor the next morning. Craig was what? About ten at the time?"

"It was a little scary the first night, but I felt safe once he lay down on the floor with me."

"He loved you so much. Remember…"

He left the rest of his thoughts unsaid. Sophie took over.

"I loved him too. He was great at playing chase."

"You were his dog all right." Billy thought about how Craig was the disciplinarian when Sophie acted up. "Remember how he'd pick you up when you did something bad, get right in your face, and give you a stern lecture on your behavior."

"I always thought he was just playing with me when he'd do that. Never realized he was trying to get me to behave differently."

As he glanced at her, something caught his eye.

"Sophie, you're wearing your collar." Sophie always wore a red dog collar.

"I always loved my collar and was able to take it with me after I left you."

"It complements your black fur."

Craig bought the collar with money he earned mowing lawns as a teenager. It was a source of pride for the youngster that he was able to do that with his own money. It was a source of pride for Billy that his son used some of his own money to do things for others. Like the time he treated his parents to a nice meal on their wedding anniversary shortly before he died. How a young man was able to do this while working for minimum wage at Target mystified Billy.

Craig, like a lot of other Millennials during the Great Recession, lived at home after he graduated from college. He saved his money in hopes of eventually moving to Charleston, South Carolina. Craig's goal was to work at the new Boeing plant in that city. Failing that, he discussed transferring to one of the Target stores there. Pride at his son's desire for independence and perseverance in working toward a goal, all the while coping with a malignant brain tumor, swelled Billy's chest.

Sophie suddenly brought him back from his reverie. "Dad! Dad! Is that a DQ sign?!"

He looked over in her direction and saw another flash of red, blue, yellow and white.

"No, sweetie. That's a Burger King sign."

"But, it looks like a DQ sign, Dad. Are you sure? Are you sure?"

"Yes, I'm sure. It's a Burger King sign. See. It's got much more yellow in it than a DQ sign has."

Billy could not help but smile despite sensing Sophie's disappointment. Her naivete was too funny not to. The image of her and Craig sharing a Peanut Buster Parfait crept into his thinking.

"You and Craig were best buddies, weren't you?"

"Oh. Craig was always the best brother ever. I missed him so much when he left us."

"You never showed it," Billy said. *Wonder if I could learn from Sophie how to deal with losing Craig?* "You seemed to take it pretty well after he died. How were you able to do it? To not feel depressed, and not question why he had to die before you?"

"Craig prepared me. He used to tell me that there was a chance he might have to leave me for a long time, but that we'd eventually get to see each other again."

This was news to Billy. *Craig never talked about death and dying with me or his mother the entire seven years he had cancer.*

"What did Craig say to you? When did he say it?"

"It was after the first time he had that terrible shaking," she said.

Billy interpreted that to mean Craig's first grand mal seizure. That event initiated seven-years of interactions with the medical industry.

"Afterwards, he sometimes talked to me when we were alone about what was going on and why he had to leave me every so often."

"What did he say?"

"He would tell me about visiting the doctor or the hospital." Craig endured many visits to the University of Virginia Health Center. He also suffered through two major neurosurgeries at that facility. "And about what they did to him."

"Was he scared?"

"Yes."

Craig never gave an inkling of being afraid to either parent, although he sometimes did vent his frustration in dealing with the medical system to his mother.

"When did he tell you these things?" Billy asked.

"Mostly at night, when we were in bed, but always when no one else was around."

"Did he worry about dying?"

"Yes."

"Do you remember much about the day Craig died?"

"I do remember the last time I saw Craig alive."

"Remember the 'passing of the hound' routine?"

Sophie nodded. This was a nightly routine wherein Billy and Craig made a humorous parody of a 'passing of the torch' by passing Sophie from father to son before the father went to bed.

"Craig wanted to stay up late, so we 'passed the hound', and he went upstairs with you to watch TV. You were the last to see him alive."

Time moved backward four years in Billy's brain. Usually up by 7:00 AM on Saturdays, that morning they assumed Craig's late night resulted in his sleeping in. At 9:00 AM, Billy told his wife that he thought he had better check on him. Images flooded Billy's consciousness: opening Craig's closed door, his son lying face down on his bed, trying to wake him only to realize something was not right. Panic. Desperation. Futilely attempting to rouse him. Crying out for his wife. Hopelessness. It was too late. Craig had died sometime during the night. Billy cried and rubbed Sophie's back as they sat on the bed and waited for the paramedics.

"You think about him every day, don't you, Dad?"

"It never gets better. Time passes, but the same hurt remains. It never gets any better, never any less hurtful. Someone once said that losing a child is a heartache that never heals." Billy struggled to see the road through his tears.

Why Not Me?

"Until you go to Heaven."

Sophie's response to Billy's heartache comment left him in a quandary. *How to respond to that? Do I even need to respond?*

He glanced in her direction and reminded himself that she was, after all, only a dog. Then he chastised himself for thinking she was 'only a dog', and finished his thoughts with *this is only a dream*.

Sophie was much more than just a dog, but as with others of her species, her concepts of life and death, Heaven and Hell, being and existence, must be pretty unsophisticated. More black-and-white, he reasoned.

How could she possibly understand the mental turmoil going on inside my head since Craig's death?

No, he would not go there. Not into that dark, dreary place with someone as simple and innocent as Sophie. Instead, he shook his head.

He asked, "Why hasn't Craig visited me in a dream himself?"

"Sometimes people are sent, but not often because it's riskier than sending pets."

"How so?"

"Let's say you tell someone that you had a weird dream where your dog Sophie visited you and talked to you. What would they say?"

"They'd laugh and say it sounded like a weird dream. Probably make a joke about me going crazy."

"Okay, but what if you tell them that you had a dream where your deceased son Craig visited you?"

Billy considered his reply. "They'd probably think I was seriously grieving., or maybe seriously hurting emotionally and mentally."

"It would be more disturbing to them, wouldn't it, than if you told them you dreamed about your dead dog? If it happened more than once, they might suspect that you were having some sort of psychological problem."

Billy nodded. "Yeah, that makes sense. There's less risk of others thinking you're going crazy if you dream about a deceased pet than a deceased loved one."

"That's part of it. There's another risk in sending Craig to visit you."

"Such as?"

"You could become dependent upon your dreams. You might live only to see your deceased loved one in your dreams, and not go on living your life. Man has free will, so sometimes he conjures up deceased loved ones in dreams on his own, but it's typically not because God sends them."

Billy nodded, again wiped some of the wetness from his eyes, but remained silent as Sophie continued.

"People need to move on. Your loved ones still alive need you. Your deceased loved ones want you to move on."

Billy thought about the many conversations he had with his wife. "Mom and I talked about it after Craig died. We both figured that we had raised Craig to overcome adversity. Look at the way he coped with his tumor. He finished three more years of college and graduated with honors. Worked at Target and was doing well there. They even used him to open a new store in Tuscaloosa. He survived two brain surgeries and seemed to be doing quite well before…"

Billy paused to wipe away more tears, then resumed.

"The thing is you don't roll over and die when you face adversity. That's what we always told Craig. I told Mom that when I die, I wouldn't want my loved ones to go into a perpetual state of grieving. I'd want them to miss me of course, to think about me once in a while, but to carry on and live a happy life. Not fall into a deep pit of depression and suicide. That's the way we raised Craig, and he would certainly think the same way. So, your Mom and I figured we needed to live our lives as we taught Craig to live his, because that's the way he would want it. It is one way of honoring him."

"I couldn't have said it better."

A black thought occurred to Billy.

"So, I take it that you're here in my dream instead of Craig so people won't think I've gone daft? It's more likely that I'll move on and live my life normally?" Billy was unable to mask the sarcasm in his last comment.

"I'm here because you haven't adjusted very well to Craig's death."

"I don't know that I'll ever adjust well to Craig's death. I expect to go to my grave with the feelings I have right now."

"You still haven't told me what's really troubling you. Are you angry? Many people get angry when a loved one dies. You never got angry after Craig died, did you?"

"No… no."

"Why not? Anger after a loved one's death is a common emotion."

"I don't really know. For some reason, I could never get mad after Craig died. Still can't."

"What *do* you feel?"

"Sadness and grief for sure, overwhelming grief sometimes."

"Yet, you've managed to carry on since Craig died."

"Yeah, I guess. If you call living with the death of your son 'carrying on'."

"You still haven't told me what's really troubling you. It's not anger, and I don't think it's fear of dying yourself."

"No, losing a child is the worst thing that can ever be done to me. Dying for me would pale beside that. And by 'that', I mean losing Craig."

"So, what is it?"

Long silence.

"I don't know. Disappointment?"

"Disappointment?"

"I guess it's disappointing that it wasn't me instead of Craig. I'm an old man. I've lived a long, happy, fulfilled life. If someone has to go, why not me? Why Craig? I would have been happy to go instead of him."

"Why not you? I wish I knew the answer to that," Sophie said as she looked upward, "but it's above my pay grade. I do know that what you feel is not uncommon among parents who have children that die before them."

"I guess I'm disappointed that whatever causes these things to happen caused it to happen the way it did." Billy paused. "But, there's something else, something else besides my disappointment that Craig and not me died."

"What is it?"

Billy pondered going into that dark, dreary place he never dared with anyone else. *How can I go there with someone as simple and innocent as Sophie?* But it was too late. He was almost there anyway.

"It's something else. It's something I dread."

"Dread? Fear can be a part of dread, but dread can also mean something else besides fear. You're talking about that something else."

"Yeah, I am."

"Dread can also be a reluctance; reluctance to do something, to meet someone, or to experience something for reasons other than fear."

Billy nodded. "Yes. That's it. Reluctance."

"Tell me what you're reluctant to experience."

"Death."

"You're reluctant to experience dying?"

"No. Dying doesn't scare me. I'm not afraid of dying. It's like I said, after Craig died, I thought that no one could do anything to me that was worse than taking my son. Losing a child is absolutely the worst thing that can happen to a parent. There will be no other thing or event in my life that ever exceeds that in terms of pain. Not even dying myself."

"Then you dread death, not dying. Why, if that's when you'll see Craig again?"

"Yeah… maybe, or maybe not."

"Maybe not? What do you mean?"

"I know I'm going to die. Everyone dies. It's inevitable, but I don't fear it. In some ways, I welcome it. But I don't know what death itself is like. What if there is no life after death? What if when we die, that's it? We just go away? Like the title of that old Peggy Lee song *Is That All There Is?* Is that all there is to life? We live sixty, seventy years, then we die and that's all there is. There is no Heaven or no Hell. We simply cease to exist. What if the atheists turn out to be right? That's why I dread death. I dread the possibility that I might never see Craig again."

Billy found he could not continue. He wiped more tears from his eyes as Sophie looked at him. I knew she wanted to jump into his lap and lick his face but wisely refrained from so doing. As luck would have it, they were at a point in the commute where traffic was stop-and-go. Billy focused on driving until he had composed himself.

"The worst part of that scenario is that we never get to see our loved ones again. I dread the thought of death because that's the way it may actually be—dying and not existing any more. Never able to be with Craig again. The thought of never seeing him, never seeing my mother, father, brother, wife, daughter, friends. I think that is the saddest thought in the world. Never seeing your loved ones after you die. Of course, the church says there is life after death, but… who knows? It's been a constant thought inside me for four years now."

I suffered during the long silence that followed. Billy's free will might take him anywhere with this reasoning. What can anyone say to someone who thinks like this? Dachshunds are known for being less than subtle in their interactions with others, probably a Teutonic personality trait. But I had to trust Sophie.

She said, "No one living really knows what actually happens after they die. All that bunkum you read about people dying and coming back from death is idle speculation. Don't believe anyone who says they died, experienced the next world, then came back to life. Their heart may have stopped beating and their lungs stopped breathing for a while, but they did not actually die. I don't care what they say they saw in the next world. They didn't actually die. The only time anyone will actually know what happens after they die is when they actually die. It's the same for you. Existence of life after death is based on pure faith alone."

"Thanks for nothing."

"I'm not finished. Hear me out. If there is any hope of staying sane and rational in this universe, it lies in hope that there is something beyond this world. Some Greater Being that has provided for something beyond this world. But you won't actually know it until you die."

Billy remained silent, prompting Sophie to take a different tack.

"Think of it this way. Although Craig died, he still lives on."

"I don't understand."

"He lives on in your heart, in his mother's heart, and in his sister's heart, just to name three. He lives on in others' hearts as well. All those whom he touched while alive."

Billy thought of many conversations, especially those at family gatherings, since Craig's death. Invariably, some story about him would be retold that would lead to a good laugh. He thought about how his daughter occasionally talks with Cricket about her Uncle Craig. As a result, the four-year old thinks of him as being alive and wonders why he does not come to visit her. It occurred to Billy that Craig truly lives on in Cricket's heart as well as the rest of the family.

"I do have to agree. Craig does live in his family's hearts. Other's hearts as well."

Billy's pause prompted Sophie to ask, "What? What else is bothering you?"

"It's like I said a while ago. If someone has to die, why Craig? Why not me? If there is a God, why would a loving God take a wonderful young man like Craig instead of me? It doesn't make sense." Billy paused to wipe his cheeks with the back of his sleeve. Sophie remained silent. She knew he would finish in his own time. He finally said, "How could anything but random chance explain taking a young man like him instead of me? Surely no loving God would do it that way. Random chance is the only way a simple mind like mine can explain why things happen that way. And that means I'll never see Craig again."

I knew the existence of chance did not preclude My existence and his seeing Craig again.

"No. It might not be that way at all," Sophie said.

"How so?"

"Maybe it's as simple as God wanted Craig with him at this time and not you."

"Why?"

"Who knows? Maybe he has some purpose for you right here right now. Maybe he just wanted Craig with him."

Engrossed in their conversation, Billy almost missed the exit to his office. A sharp swerve into the outside lane sent Sophie flying. She bounced off the passenger door and back onto the seat. Billy could feel daggers in the stare she gave him.

"Thank goodness this is the first and only time I'll have to make this trip with you," she said.

"Sorry, but my exit kind of snuck up on us. You okay?"

As Sophie nodded, Billy saw something he knew would mollify her.

"Look, there's the DQ I told you about."

At that announcement, Sophie's head popped up, and she began closely monitoring their progress. As Billy pulled into the DQ entrance, Sophie jumped up, putting her front paws on the car's center console. She remained quiet as they pulled into the drive-thru. Billy shouted his order into the speaker.

"A Peanut Buster Parfait and a medium coffee, please."

"Dad, I can't wait," Sophie's front paws repeatedly bounced up and down on the console in a frenzy of excitement as Billy pulled up to the window. "It's been way too long since I've had a PBP."

"I would've thought you'd have a PBP every day in Heaven."

"No, they don't do it that way."

"Why not?"

"It's like that old *Twilight Zone* I watched with you. The one where the bad guy dies and goes to a place where they give him everything he wants. He thinks he's in Heaven, but it turns out he's in Hell."

"Yeah. I remember that one. One of my favorites. Turns out that having everything your way really is Hell. Everything the same every day? Totally predictable. You get bored." Billy added a tease. "Although I can't imagine a dachshund ever getting bored having its own way."

"Har, har, har. Very funny."

At that moment, the drive-thru window opened, and their order was passed to them. Billy put both items in the console's cup holders, paid the bill, and pulled ahead.

"Can I have it now? I can't wait! I can't wait!"

Billy obliged by parking in an empty slot in the DQ parking lot. He uncovered Sophie's treat and placed it back into the cup holder. The little dog put her front paws on the center console and began to gorge herself.

Typical dachshund.

Resolution

Inadequate gentle shaking at first had to be followed by that more vigorous, which achieved its goal. Billy's wife stood over him when his eyes finally opened.

"You've done it again. This is the third time this week you've fallen asleep at your desk."

"Mmmmm. So, what's new?" Billy sarcastically replied while muffling a yawn. " What time is it?"

"After six."

"Wow. Sophie gets around. Looks like she decided to visit me this time."

"You had a dream about Sophie?"

"Yeah. What a doozy. I'm back in Virginia, doing that god awful commute to DC, stop to pick up a slug, and lo and behold, it's Sophie. She makes the commute with me as my slug."

"That must've been interesting."

"Weird is more like it. She talked to me."

"Sophie talking? Now, I've heard everything. She never talks to me in my dreams. What did she say? Did she sound like Scooby-Doo? You need to avoid leftover kung pao chicken before bedtime from now on."

"She sounded like Marlene Dietrich. We talked about times when she was alive, about Craig, things like that."

I knew Billy's wife understood how difficult it was for him to talk about their son.

"Sounds like a heavy dream."

Billy nodded. "The weirdest part of the dream was after we pulled into the DQ near the office. I ordered her a Peanut Buster Parfait."

"I bet she devoured that."

"Sophie just sat there, gorging herself on her PBP while I cried. That's how the dream ended when you woke me up. Sophie stuffing her face and me crying."

"Why were you crying?"

"Thinking about Craig, how he still lives in Cricket's heart. You know how she thinks Uncle Craig is alive and wonders when he will come visit her. He is alive in her heart."

"Yes, he truly is."

I knew one thing still vexed Billy.

"Too bad Craig can't live in the hearts of everyone, just like he does ours. I wish I could figure out a way to bring him into everyone's heart."

In Everyone's Heart

I sat on My throne, about to read something when Sophie slowly approached. Her sluggishness resulted from having just finished an intense game of chase with Craig. The poor little thing panted. The look on her face said *I'm tired. Hold me.* After all, it was her nap time. The game resulted from My suggestion that she engage in some activity to offset all the calories she put on eating that Peanut Buster Parfait.

I put what I was about to read aside, picked her up, and placed her in My lap. She snuggled into one of the folds of My robe, a picture of contentment, sighing deeply to prove it.

"You did well, Miss Sophie."

She was too tired to do anything requiring effort, so she simply moaned softly. Her eyelids drooped. I scratched her neck. She loves it when I scratch underneath her red collar.

"Your dad seems more at ease now. I feel much better Myself at seeing some of his mental anguish lessened."

Sophie gave me a happy 'grrr' of contentment.

I teased her, "Looks like your dad has indeed figured out a way to bring Craig into many others' hearts."

Sophie lifted her head slightly and gave me a perplexed look. I knew what she thought. *Okay. How about getting on with it and telling me how?*

"It's pretty ingenious. A very imaginative idea if I do say so Myself."

Sophie sat up, eager to find out more.

"Here. I'll show you." I picked My reading materials back up. "Let me turn to the first page of what I was just starting to read before you came, and you'll understand how Craig will indeed live on in many hearts for ages to come."

Turn the page to understand how.

THE SEQUESTERED NOOK

By Craig Johnson

He always loved the name, The Sequestered Nook, for it symbolized everything great about the shop: love of books and separation from life's tedium. It was a hideaway for people weary of daily commutes, fights with spouses, or worry over the future. Anyone could escape and find solace between leather bound books and fraying paperbacks. Books of every genre were welcomed at the Nook: classic literature, fantasy, thrillers, young adult, and science fiction; even foreign editions aligned its deep mahogany walls. The store sold both old trade-ins and brand-new bestsellers. In fact, there was only one true criterion that the store respected: sell only fiction. Literature was the escape route from reality. Any person—rich or poor, old or young, successful or not—could become someone, or something else inside a great novel. To varying degrees, this was the reason that the Nook had such faithful patronage. They would make extra time to go there rather than to the larger superstore that was closer and cheaper. The Nook was that cozy inn at the end of a long, cold road that served guests warm refreshments, a gentle pillow, and a good book. After a relaxing time, the people would leave the shop, rejuvenated and ready to handle that winding road.

But to one Nook patron, life was a harsh desert, and books were an oasis.

People view life in three different ways. Some see it as a challenge to overcome, with each obstacle only strengthening their character.

Others find it easy and walk through life with little trouble or worry. The final group view life as something mysterious, complex, terrifying, and sickening. Merrill was born with this final group's vision. A natural loner, Merrill was born with an uncaring mother and no knowledge of his true father. Growing up, he found himself outside of any social circle. No one wanted to befriend him, and as years passed Merrill consequently decided he did not need to have friends. Not needing others was a fantasy he created, a narrative that did not match reality. In truth, Merrill was desperately alone. Merrill tried not to, but sometimes wished he had never been born.

Merrill contemplated suicide on several occasions during high school. He would plan out the event out in his mind. Like a stage play, Merrill could see his tragic life unfold before the audience. He imagined his peers, the ones that rejected him, talking, gossiping, whispering, about the boy who was so odd. Then after his death, they would come to realize their mistake, their ignorance, and become ashamed. His legacy would be born after death, and that gave Merrill some measure of relief.

Perhaps Merrill would have gone through his suicide… were it not for his talent.

One Thursday afternoon Merrill was reading. The book was called Transgressions of the Transgressor. It was a novel about a man living in Alaska who becomes an oil tycoon during the early 20th Century. He read the line, 'A low snow flake touched his cracked lips,' and suddenly Merrill felt a strange sensation. He felt a cold rush of air… and suddenly Merrill was there. Not just there in his mind. He was there physically. His body was in Alaska, not sitting here in his usual chair in the library. He looked around at wild Alaskan wilderness. There were steel-silver mountain tops, brushed slightly by eagles painting the sky. There was the cold air that sucked oxygen from lungs. There was not the reality of here. In short, Merrill was actually in the novel itself. And even more fantastic, he was no longer Merrill but the protagonist of the story. He looked down at his own person and saw a stranger's body. He was tall, rugged, and now wore an animal hide. Merrill was no longer himself but rather the embodiment of a writer's vision.

Merrill should have been scared. He should have been terrified, jarred, ill at ease, questioning, or have tried to rationalize. He was not. It was a strange sensation, something both odd and new for Merrill. He felt a sense of finally belonging. It was like coming to a home in which he had never lived, a place both foreign and native. As if all of the sudden Merrill had found his niche in the world. It felt more than right. It felt natural.

Merrill quit contemplating suicide. He did not have to worry about people, his dysfunctional family, or his lack of potential. Merrill believed he was given a gift that others should envy. People wish for more, strive for greater, and are often disappointed with their reality. They take expensive vacations to leave their own world and pay workers to treat them like someone special. Now Merrill had a passport for the greatest of destinations.

In the beginning it was difficult for Merrill to both understand and, more importantly, replicate his gift. The first experience lasted mere minutes before Merrill slipped back into reality. He sat in that library chair for hours trying to get back into the literary world, but to no avail. It wasn't until two weeks later that he again transported. As with the first, the second transportation occurred without warning. One minute he was sitting on the school's steps, the next he was onboard a ship sailing the Pacific Ocean. After that incident Merrill worked even harder to perfect his talent. Eventually he was able to enter and exit literary worlds at will. His ability to reality jump became a sixth sense, a muscle that grew stronger with time.

Increasingly, Merrill spent more time in the realm of fiction than in reality. Things in life that used to stifle him were no longer bothersome. Hazing from peers could be easily forgotten in a few lines of literature. His mother's dismissive attitude, once a source of great pain, was now a mild annoyance. Merrill could spend long stretches of time inside a book. Hours became days. Days turned into weeks, then months, and finally years. Merrill had free will to walk around the novel's landscape, assume a character's body and life, and exist within the novel's span of time. But no matter how long he inhabited a novel, Merrill would always return to reality having only lost a minute of time. Life was still here after every trip from there.

Merrill graduated from high school without much recognition. He had decent enough grades, but he did not have any desire to pursue college or a career. Merrill only wanted more time to spend with books. It was Merrill's mother who forced him to do something with his life. She gave him an ultimatum: go to school, get a job, or move out. He needed a purpose, or at least a reason to leave the house. Merrill decided to attend a community college, but he only took English courses. His advisor told Merrill that he needed other courses in order to graduate. But Merrill was not interested in having a degree, only to remain separated from reality as long as possible. After two years, Merrill left the college, having taken all the available literary classes.

It was then that reality loomed over Merrill. His mother, weary of having him in the house, told Merrill to leave and begin his own life. He would need to make a living, have a place to stay, food to eat, and, more importantly, money to buy books. Distraught, Merrill knew that he needed a job. He would have to become one of those most depressing sights: a working man.

The thought of obtaining a steady job terrified Merrill. Lack of work skills and talent limited his options. His love of books gave him an insight. Why not work in a book shop? His first choice was The Sequestered Nook, as it was a place he frequented during high school. The Nook had not changed since his last visit before graduation. It was an old shop, sandwiched between a pizza shop and a dress boutique. The place was so old that the owner had never bothered to setup a website. This was a problem as Merrill had hoped to apply on-line without having to interview in person. He summoned his courage and entered the Nook.

Merrill walked around the shop's door for several minutes before entering. A girl stood behind the counter. He had seen her before and remembered that she was the proprietor's daughter. Merrill remembered seeing her working with her father and helping with customers as she learned the business. He had not seen her since his graduation. Back then she was a gangly little girl whose head was too big for her small shoulders. But she was a natural with the customers. She had that nice mixture of precociousness and sincerity with an inviting face. As he approached, Merrill noticed a large wooden plaque mounted on the wall above the counter. It contained the following quote. "The love of learning, the sequestered nooks, And all the sweet serenity of books— Henry Wadsworth Longfellow.

"Hey, can I help you find something?" the girl asked.

Merrill mumbled his response, asked if the shop was hiring.

“We do have an opening in sales. Here’s an application that you can fill out,” Clare said, handing him a piece of paper from under the cash register. She was roughly his age, maybe a year or so younger. She had grown in those few years, replacing her awkward gait with a more graceful pose. Her face was more round than angular and was more welcoming than alluring. Panic seized Merrill’s body as he took the application. He disliked talking to others, more so when it involved something official such as applying for a job. He mumbled a thank you and quickly filled out the paper before returning it to Clare wordlessly. She later told her father about the odd young man who asked for a job.

“Oh, I saw him earlier. I know him,” Clare’s father, Cyril, said. They were closing up the shop.

“You know him?” Clare asked incredulously.

“Yeah, he’s been here before, remember? He used to go over to the chairs in the back and read just a few pages at a time. Hardly ever bought anything. That was some years ago now, I think, when he was going to the other high school.”

“He’s a strange one. Kinda creepy too.”

“Well, then you’re not going to like what I have to say.”

Clare had seen that look before, “What? Are you seriously thinking about hiring him?”

“Hon, listen. We do need some help here, and I mean more than some part-time high-schooler. We need another full-time salesman.”

"But Dad..."

Cyril held up a patient hand. Clare was often too quick to prejudge for her own good. "I'm only talking about an interview. I remember him reading a lot of books. And not just science fiction or fantasy, but every genre of fiction. You know my motto: only –"

"Only fiction," finished Clare. She did love her father, even if he was often too sentimental for his own good.

"Correct. Besides my dear Clare, hiring him doesn't mean we can't fire him."

Merrill did interview for the position—a poor interview at best. His communication skills became apparent as he mumbled and fumbled his words. Despite this, Cyril was impressed by the young man's knowledge of books. Merrill answered questions about a wide variety of novels from many genres and time periods. This was a rare trait. Previously, Cyril hiring choices had been primarily limited to high school kids whose literary knowledge only included the latest teenage thriller craze and graphic novels. He reasoned Merrill could be an excellent asset for the shop, if only he could learn to communicate. Despite his own misgivings and Clare's warning, Cyril hired Merrill on a provisional basis.

Initially, Merrill was not good at customer service. He was nervous around people and often busied himself needlessly when asked a question. Clare tried to use this as an excuse for terminating Merrill. “He actually runs away from people, Dad. Just fire him, please.”

Cyril patiently replied, “That’s why you train him. Teach him how to sell a product. If you ever want to take over this shop, then you’re going to have to learn how to manage people. Even those you don’t like.”

Clare reluctantly complied and spent the next week trying to show Merrill how to interact with other people. “You should always ask customers, ‘Can I help you find something?’ Don’t be afraid of them. Be proactive, take charge.”

“Okay,” mumbled Merrill.

“What’s that?” asked Clare, her voice audibly tinged with frustration. “Speak up. Enunciate. Nobody can hear you with your head down like that.”

“Okay,” Merrill replied before he busied himself again. Clare shook her head in frustration. Merrill hated this job. It was even more stressful than school. He had not come here to interact with people. These people came into the Sequestered Nook with their own realities, baggage, mishaps, accomplishments, trials, rewards, and lives. He did not want the responsibility of having to deal with all that. He felt helpless and not in control. He did not want to be involved in the reality inside the Sequestered Nook. He wanted to go into his other worlds.

Merrill could not escape this new reality. He had spent, and could still spend years in other worlds which books provided. However, he always returned to the reality he really disliked. He knew he needed to make this reality livable. He had to make this reality work for him. He figured he could make the best of his current situation. It did afford him access to a lot of good books.

The first three weeks were the most difficult for Merrill. He was thrust into an unwanted job and life. Clare kept expecting her father to admit his error and terminate Merrill. But somehow Merrill improved his attitude. He would begin the day pensive with a mixture of regret and acceptance. Then somewhere around midday, after having stocked the store with new arrivals and sorted the previous day's trade-ins, his mood would improve, and he became ever so slightly sociable toward customers. He listened to Clare's training and began to implement her strategies. Each day improved. The days became weeks, and by the end of three months Merrill had become something of a salesman.

Merrill's knowledge of books and authors exceeded that which Clare initially suspected. She realized it was not that he simply knew a lot about many authors and plots. Merrill had a way of describing books that was eerily sagacious. He possessed an ability to connect with customers when they talked about books. She overheard a conversation between Merrill and a customer about *To Kill a Mockingbird.*

The customer said, “Oh I remember when I first read it. I just loved the way Harper Lee wrote that book. I felt so—"

“Secure,” Merrill interjected. “I know. When you read it, you get that feeling of being home. You know that you’re safe, even when it seems dark. And I mean dark. Like the part where the men come to the jail. You truly feel fear when they come for Tom. And even though you’re afraid, you’re somehow self-assured because you know that Atticus is there. You know that you’ll be safe.”

“Exactly!”

“You know another book that I got that same feeling from was…” Merrill stopped speaking, immediately walked to one of the store’s aisles, and came back with a copy of *A Tree Grows in Brooklyn*. The customer left with it in her shopping back. Many customers began asking Merrill for his advice on what to read, knowing he could intuitively sense what they would like.

Every month Merrill improved his selling ability. A confident tone replaced his mumbling, he stood straighter, and he began to initiate conversation with customers. The change was dramatic. But it was also beneficial and soon the shop experienced a significant revenue boost. Even Clare had to admit that Merrill was a good asset for the Nook. She surmised that Merrill could excel if put in his natural element. Apparently this element was literature. There were always four or five books under his arms in the morning, usually different ones from the previous day. Clare, who digested nearly three books a week, could not fathom how Merrill found time to read so much.

"How do you read them so fast?" she asked one day, when they were closing up the store. It was a question that nagged at her. She even wondered if he was not reading books in their entirety.

"Oh, it's all a matter of finding time, I guess," he mumbled, something that he had not done in several months.

"Really? Because I read a lot. In fact, I used to read so much that my dad had to pull me away just to eat. But still, I don't seem to come close to you. I mean, you have several different books every day, and some are quite long."

"I… I don't know how I do it," Merrill began to fumble. "I… I just love books, you know. It's no big deal."

"I'm not accusing you of anything. I'm just curious. I've had customers ask what you read, and I just say, 'everything'. How do you do it?"

"I just… I'll just go and get the backroom squared away," Merrill said as he walked away. He developed a small amount of perspiration on his lips. He hated himself for leaving like that. He was doing well at the shop and in his relations with Clare. He even enjoyed talking to her. Cyril occasionally heard laughter only to find the two of them to be its source. But this time, he felt like she was being accusatory. No one knew of Merrill's gift, and he wanted no one to know. Clare would certainly never believe it. She would think him insane and throw him out of the Nook. And Merrill didn't want that, now.

Life is difficult. Some people have little control over nor certainty in life. An old man examines his life with more yearning than appreciation. He sees instances where he could have been smarter in his thinking and stronger in his courage—a better man. But he is not. He is poorer, weaker, ugly, broken. He wishes rather than brags.

That did not have to be true for Merrill. He was a lucky man. Merrill did not have to worry about his life, his future, or dwell on his past. Inside a book, he could live a better life than his own. Books were more than a fun adventure to Merrill. They were his security. An author is the doctor who examines life, finds its faults, and provides answers to improve a reader's understanding. An author is like a parent to the reader. In a book, Merrill did not have to worry about making wrong decisions. He would never be a loser or look back with regret and disgust.

Merrill reached his first year of working at The Sequestered Nook. "We should do something for him," Cyril said. "After all, no one else has lasted longer than a few months."

"Well… What did you have in mind?"

"I was going to ask you that. You know more about him than I."

Clare's cheeks flushed, "How's that?"

"Well, I've seen the two of you talk frequently. Especially in the evenings, while we're closing up shop."

"Come on, he's an employee, so of course I talk to him, even when we close. You're also his boss, you talk to him."

"Not as much as you," he replied.

"Well, he's not much of a talker, you know. Just about books, and even that's only with customers."

"Oh, I don't know. I seem to remember you two laughing about something just yesterday."

Clare thought back to that moment. She had no idea that her father was there, or that he saw anything. "Oh, come on. That was nothing. I really don't know that much about him. He's a loner and aloof." It was odd how sometimes Merrill could be conversational, even slightly charming, and then the next day be back inside his own private world.

But the celebration never occurred. Clare came to the store early one morning to find that her father was not there. Clare should have been alarmed. Cyril usually opened the shop. But she decided to ignore this oddity and continued with her tasks. Cyril still had not come in by the afternoon, so Clare tried to call him. He did not answer. Clare closed the Nook and went to her father's house. He sat slumped over at the kitchen table, dead.

Massive heart attack. That was the coroner's ruling. There was no obvious cause for the attack. Cyril was healthy and kept an active lifestyle. It was simply his time.

A week after the funeral, Clare spoke with Merrill. She said, "I don't know what I'm going to do." The Sequestered Nook had been closed since Cyril's death. She hesitated, being doubtful she could bear returning to the Nook.

"About the store?" Merrill asked. He was saddened to hear of Cyril. Merrill had grown fond of the Nook's owners. Cyril always treated Merrill fairly and was patient while he learned to be a good salesman. Merrill even agreed to give small speech at the funeral, thanking Cyril for seeing potential in him. That Friday morning, after the funeral, Merrill received a call from Clare, asking him to join her at the shop.

"It's going to be so hard to run this place without him. Things were okay financially but now without Dad..." The Nook was a uniquely profitable shop. In an age when more and more people read books on a screen, a successful physical bookstore was rare. "He was so important to this store. People loved him. That's why we've been in business so long. Ever since Amazon, mom-and-pop bookstores have been shutting down. But not The Sequestered Nook. It was him, Merrill. It was Dad."

Merrill glanced at the plaque mounted on the wall and silently read its words as he sat with Clare at one of the tables near the window. He looked back at her. She looked sad, and this troubled Merrill. He did not like to see her this way. He wanted her to be happy again. "People love you too," he said. "You're just as important to this place as he was."

"No, it's… honestly, I don't know if I can run this store without him. I mean everywhere I'll see him. The memory might be too painful." Clare thought about the other employees she would have to terminate if she decided to shut down.

"But it doesn't have to be that way Clare," Merrill replied. He looked at her eyes and saw pain behind them. Life was hurting her, and he wanted it to stop. He desperately wished that he could do something to protect her. "Look, think of it this way. He's gone from this world, but he's still here, in the shop. He's everywhere, in the bookshelves, the tables, right down to that clunky cash register. And that's a good thing. That means he'll be here whenever you're here. You can never lose him again."

Clare smiled at his words. Even now, after working with him for a year, Merrill still found ways to surprise her. "Wow," she wiped her eyes, "That's nice. Really nice, Merrill. Thank you."

"It's nothing," Merrill said as he saw a glimmer of light return to her eyes. She was comforted by him, a pleasing thought in itself. He could not remember being this proud of himself in a long time, if ever. "And I mean it too."

Clare thought back to her father's last wish—a celebration for Merrill's first anniversary.

"You know before, um… this past two weeks, my father wanted to do something. For you."

"Me?" Merrill felt anxiety in his stomach. He did not like it when others talked about him. He hated attracting attention to himself.

"Well, you know that it's been a year since you were hired, and Dad and I felt that you should have some sort of celebration in your honor."

"Celebration?"

"Yeah, you know. Like a first-year anniversary kind of thing. You're actually the Nook's longest working employee, besides me."

Merrill was uncomfortable with this. He had never tracked his time with the Nook. But they had. They had been counting the days, the weeks, the months. They had been discussing him, talking about his performance, judging him. Drops of sweat appeared on Merrill's brow. He said, "Well, that's not important."

"Oh, stop it," Clare said, lightly tapping his shoulder. "It is a big deal. It was to Dad. It is to me. We both thought you were doing great."

"No, it's not really a big deal," Merrill mumbled. He was not angry at Cyril or Clare for talking about him, only that they had done so behind his back. The thought of being judged by others made him nervous. He began to re-experience a feeling of lack of control over his life. He suddenly experienced a paranoid thought, 'If I was doing so well, why did they talk about me behind my back. Maybe I haven't been doing as well as I thought?' Despite his emotional growth over the last year, Merrill's past insecurities still simmered. Did others still saw him as the failure? He frequently felt himself to be a failure in the past.

Clare bit her bottom lip. Merrill was the reason she had not immediately closed the shop. Merrill, not the Nook's other employees, had made her look forward to work each day. She hated the thought of running the shop without her father, but she hated running it without Merrill even more. She said, "I want to talk to you about something."

Merrill hands fidgeted. "What is it?"

"Part of me wants to close the shop. But another part of me doesn't. As I said, I can't imagine running this place without Dad, but that's because I don't want to run it by myself. Do you understand?"

"I'm not sure that I do."

Clare hesitated then said, "What I mean is… I was wondering if, uh… you'd like, or consider… being a… well, a partner in the Nook. We could work something out."

Merrill's thoughts exploded. 'Oh God, it's even worse. No, no, no. I don't want that, not that responsibility.' Clare's offer was too much, too soon for the maturing young man. He said, "A partner? You mean a partner to run the shop with you?"

Clare suddenly felt embarrassed, not knowing why. "Well, yes. I mean, you work well here, customers love you. I think that we could maybe be a good team together."

Merrill thought, 'Team, together! What if I screw up, again? No. This is too much, I'm not ready.' His communication skills reverted to a simple shrug of his shoulders.

Clare could see him slinking back into his shell. "Look, Merrill. You've done really well here. You've proven yourself more than capable…"

Merrill's negative thoughts continued as she spoke. 'No, I haven't. No, I'm not. I can't do this.'

"I thought that you might want this. A promotion, you know, being a co-owner of a shop. Isn't that what you want?"

Merrill was visibly sweating. "I… I don't… Clare, I just don't…"

"What? What is it?"

"I have to go." Even before the words exited his mouth, Merrill turned and abruptly left the Nook. He went home that night to his small apartment, furnished with cheap furniture but filled with books. He struggled to regain control his psyche. It was too much, too fast, and too soon. He had grown fond of his job. True, he had grown comfortable with the store, Clare, and her father. But this was not a good life. Not the one he had thought he wanted. It wasn't one of the fantastic worlds in which he lived many times in his books. In these, he had lived glamorously, expensively, confidently, successfully. If he stayed at the Nook, then he would live a… what kind of a life? A life where he just sold books? A life with people? With

Clare? That could be good, but it could also be terrible. He just didn't know. He thought, 'I'll mess it up. It'll mess me up. No, I can't do it. I can't risk it. At best, I could just be a simple person. A ferryman for other travelers like the ferryman across the River Styx.' In a book… a great novel, Merrill could have a great life.

His thoughts continued. 'I could do it. Permanently leave this world and never return. I know that I have it in me. Just open a book, transport, and stay there.' Merrill knew that he could change his situation permanently. He could read one final book. However, he knew he would never be able to return after doing so. He would be locked into another world. Merrill could envision it—his body, lying comatose in the chair, not being found for days or even weeks. He would certainly die in the real world. But none of that would matter. His mind, his soul, would be elsewhere. Forever free from this world, locked into one more magnificent.

'What book? Which one to use to forever leave this realm?' Merrill had read thousands of books. He witnessed stunning stories with glamorous characters. 'This book must be different. I need a great book.' One that he had revisited many times came to mind. It was enjoyable as well as a story expansive enough to accommodate his existence for eternity. Most importantly, the ending had to be phenomenal.

He chose *Transgressions of the Transgressor* as his final vehicle to explore another world. It was lengthy, nearly eleven hundred pages. The story spanned over eighty years and was set in many countries. Its protagonist starts out as a poor fisherman and becomes a famous oil tycoon. It would be perfect. Merrill had read this book several times and always enjoyed its story. Varied landscapes, characters, and sensations gave him life. He thought, 'I will do this. I will go away, and never return. I will now begin my life. My new, perfect life.'

Merrill immediately opened the book and opened it to a random page. He read out loud, "Abel was not the largest son born in the village, but he was certainly the loudest, and it would later become this trait that would define not only him, but also the rest of the world—"

Suddenly, Merrill was in the book's Alaskan wilderness, feeling its cold chill. He felt alive. He felt safe. Merrill looked at himself. He was now Abel, a young boy wearing an old heavy coat and thick boots. He stood in a wild landscape, breathing cold air. A man approached and said, "Understand me, son. We are the richest men in this world. You see that sky?"

"Yes, Papa," Merrill said, having now assumed the identity of the man's son, Abel.

"That sky is ours. It belongs to us. We own it. No one can ever take away what is yours, understand me."

As the fictitious Abel had done in the book, Merrill smiled a big, toothy grin. This part of the book was nice. Jonah, his character's father, was still alive. He was the father with which

Merrill always wished he been had been blessed. It was a warming sensation, and one that he desperately needed.

Merrill timelessly wandered the novel's landscape in this manner, reliving every moment he had previously read. He relived the birth of his little sister, a hunting trip with his dog, his father's kind advice on life and love. Merrill felt no regret in his decision not to become a partner in The Sequestered Nook.

One day, Jonah said, "We are taking your uncle with us today. He needs to learn how to be a better man, so you must be patient."

Merrill looked up. He remembered this was the fishing trip in which Jonah would be killed by his brother, Abraham. He in turn would marry his widowed sister-in-law as in *Hamlet*. Merrill always felt pain reading this part. It was an extremely painful experience, feeling Abel's pain as his father was murdered. This pain would be followed by Abraham's cruelty. Abel's mother, would be forced to marry Abraham and would endure physical and mental abuse. Abel's older siblings would leave Abraham's house, while his younger siblings remained to suffer. Merrill remembered how terrible that part of the book was.

'But does it have to be?' he thought.

Merrill wondered if he could somehow alter the story. He had never tried this before, never having a need to do so. Authors always knew what was best for the story, so why try altering that which he was reading? Merrill experienced conflicting thoughts. ‘Can it be possible? Can I change the outcome and have Jonah live? What would happen?’

Merrill wanted to say, “No Papa. Don’t take him with us. He only wants Mamma for himself!”

Instead, Abel said, “Yes, Papa.”

Merrill tried again, but words only resounded in his mind. “Papa, please. Do not go onto that boat, you’ll die!”

Instead, Abel walked with Jonah and said, “Look, Papa. It’s Uncle Abraham!”

Merrill could not stop thinking, ‘No, Papa! I want to stop him. Stop Jonah. Stop!’

Jonah, still looking over the ocean that he considered home, gave a nonchalant wave at his brother. It was going to be good. Jonah felt at peace with himself. He looked at his son, the one that he always cared for most of all and said, “Son.” He wanted to say more, but words eluded him.

Abraham walked up to the boat and said, “Nice day Jonah. I believe we will have safe sailing on this morning.”

Merrill thought, ‘I must stop him. Why can’t I do so?’ Merrill tried to move his body away. He wanted to do something, anything, to stop the story from continuing. But nothing happened. Abel walked with his father on to the boat.

Merrill tried again. And again. He tried to change the unchangeable, but this was Abel’s world and not a world where a spectator got to decide events. Merrill felt the anxiety watching Jonah walk around the boat with Abraham. It would not be long before he would hear a splash as Jonah's body fell into the ocean.

Jonah told Abel to go back to the stern and check the nets. He did, and they were fine. He thought that everything seemed okay for the moment. Maybe his father would survive with enough money to make everything better. He said, "Papa, I've got the nets right here."

But his thoughts again turned negative. 'You fool. Jonah's going to be killed. Stay with him!' He wanted to warn Jonah but could not. He saw Abraham turning to Jonah on the other side of the boat and expected the worst. 'No! Not now! No! Please hear me!' Merrill was unable to move, unable to do anything.

Suddenly, Merrill experienced something he never expected—fear of certainty. In this book, life would turn out glamorous, fun, engaging, stimulating, and rich. But he would also feel pain of loss and betrayal. He would have no recourse. It was like watching a needle slowly enter into your eye. Knowing the inevitable is worse than facing the unpredictable. He thought, 'I've made a mistake.'

Suddenly, Merrill wanted out. He wanted to leave, and never return. He never wanted to live inside of a book. He wanted something more. He wanted to make choices, mistakes, even if it meant failure. He wanted something real.

But this was impossible. He had made his decision. He had made it so that he could never return, just as he had desired. He thought, 'This is the end. My end. My life as Merrill has concluded.'

With this thought, Merrill saw Jonah look at Abraham, seeing who his brother really was. Realizing his mistake, Jonah said, "Abraham, I never thought you would betray me."

Abraham looked coldly into Jonah's eyes and said, "You were always a fool. Now, what happens is not my fault."

+ +

The next morning after Merrill's journey to another world, Clare walked to the Nook. She noticed none of the urban landscape as she walked. Has she had been too forward? Had she scared Merrill? Had she had pushed him away from both her and her world? He seemed to have disappeared into another world. Clare couldn't explain her feelings. Would Merrill cease to exist in her world? She thought he might never call or write to explain where he had gone. She decided to close the Nook but only after the remaining employees had found other jobs. It hurt her to think that The Sequestered Nook would never being enjoyed again.

Cyril's passion for books kept him sane after his wife died. He often told Clare that it was the job of an author to explain life and to give the reader a perception of the world that made it a little safer. She always envied her father's ability to see better of the world through literature. Merrill did this. His unusual charm derived from a nearly child-like appreciation of books. That appreciation motivated Clare's hope that together, she and Merrill might have done something great. But that was not going to happen now. She knew that it was over.

A familiar voice behind her interrupted her walking reverie. It said, "Morning, Clare."

Clare looked over her shoulder to see the person she least expected. His hands held two cups of coffee. She said, "Merrill? I thought you weren't coming back. After last night…"

"I know how I must have appeared and I'm very sorry about that. I guess I've never had anyone who could show me that there is more to life than my books. I guess I just got scared. It's foolish, and childish. I know that now. But I've had some time to think things over, and if you're still interested, I would more than love it, if… maybe we could work together, and make the Nook something truly special."

Merrill paused, his emotions alternating between fear and excitement. He had never felt so uncertain and yet, so secure.

Clare looked him over. With a smile, she took one of the coffees from his hand. As they entered the Nook, they toasted. Afterwards, she said, "When we open, we have to get on with ordering the new Hector book. The reviews are really spectacular. I've been thinking about reading it myself. What about you?"

Glancing at the Longfellow quote on the plaque, Merrill said, “I’ve been thinking about doing something in addition to reading.”

“Oh?”

“Yeah. I’ve been reading a lot for a long time. It’s about time I do something else.”

“Really? Like what?”

Merrill’s smile extended from ear to ear. He teased, “Something much more adventurous than reading.”

“Out with it. Like what?”

“Like writing.”

Acknowledgement

Thanks to my Beta Readers: Rachell Berry, Amanda Perry, Erica Talley, Aaron Friend, Jessica Fletcher, Alannah Evans, Jordan Eagles, and Crystal Anne Casey. Their comments and suggestions proved very helpful. Thanks also to my editor Macie Pigg as well as Alannah Evans, who helped with the book's cover. Finally, thanks to Dr. Tammy Winner at University of North Alabama who arranged to have the aforementioned individuals help me.

About the Author

Billy Johnson lives in Florence, Alabama. He grew up in Panama City, Florida and attended the University of the South in Sewanee, Tennessee. Shortly after graduation, he married Linda Reed. Billy's forty-one-year career as a healthcare executive, half of that as an officer in the United States Navy Medical Service Corps, included seventeen moves around the country before he retired in 2015. He and Linda have a daughter who lives with her family in Virginia. Besides writing, he spends much of his time traveling with his wife. Billy has published one other novel, THE CASSEROLE LADIES (ISBN: 978-1-7374282-0-6), which he co-authored with Linda. The book is available on Amazon in paperback or eBook or through Ingram in paperback. You can visit Billy's Facebook page at https://www.facebook.com/Billy4GoodBooks.

www.ingramcontent.com/pod-product-compliance
Lightning Source LLC
Chambersburg PA
CBHW061205210726
48294CB00006B/1762

* 9 7 8 1 7 3 7 4 2 8 2 1 3 *